When Love Meets Lust

Stephanie Cross

Disclaimer: The characters in this book are entirely fictional. Any resemblance to actual persons living or dead is entirely coincidental.

ISBN: 978-1-9999749-0-9

First Edition

This book is dedicated to my mother, Denise. Thank you for everything.

STEPHANIE CROSS

CHAPTER 1

Love. Simple and pure. And unobtainable. For me anyway. Any potential Prince Charming within a 30 mile radius is either gay or spoken for. Only the frogs are left. The slimy, creepy frogs.

One-eyed Bill, the postman, is starting to look like a potential catch, even with his Captain Pugwash features and his Cornish accent. I don't know where the accent comes from. I don't think he has been any further than Epping Forest.

But needs must. Perhaps if I fake a peg-leg and get a parrot Bill will start finding me attractive too. Christ, I really am desperate. Fortunately, my twin sister Martha chooses this moment of deliberation to shout into my face.

'Stop staring into space you doughnut and just get up and dance.' She pulls at my arms, forcing me to my feet. 'Oh come on, this is our leaving party before we head Down Under…In the words of Prince…let's party like its 1999.'

I can't be bothered to tell her that in 1999, when we were nine, partying consisted of eating jam sandwiches and drinking fizzy pop. This particular party is definitely not like that. As I shuffle from foot to foot, trying to engage with the music, I look around at our collective and sigh. I love them all. But they make the Addams Family look normal.

At the far end of the living room, Mum and Dad are serving pina colada, in the belief that it is as popular a cocktail in 2016 as it was in 1986. They are working from a makeshift bar, and Grandad Shane is sitting just to the left of it sucking sherbet lemons and looking miserable. Next to him is Grandma Betsy, with her pencilled eyebrows drawn in so high she looks in a state of permanent shock. She also has quite a severe blue rinse, reminiscent of Dame Edna Everage.

Aunty Libby, my Mum's sister, is waving her arms around in the middle of the room. At 53 she's two years older than Mum, but as a reaction to her divorce from Uncle Kevin, who ran off with a younger woman, she has taken to dressing like a 23 year old, with peroxide-blonde hair and so much make-up she makes Chuckie the Clown look pasty. Ageing does not look like much fun to me.

Our old school friends are here too. Dave, Rosie, Si and Mel. We all went to the same primary school and all our parents are a little on the crazy side. I remember when we all went to Si's 14th birthday party and his parents thought it would be a good idea for us to sing 'Kumbaya' several times to him in the voice of David Beckham as an alternative to singing 'Happy Birthday.'

I'll miss these guys. We have lots of shared memories. Lovely memories. Memories of graduating university, spending long summer holidays cycling around Epping Forest and enjoying the sunshine on our backs as we whizzed through the green leafy landscape. Days of just being free and enjoying each other's company. Not so carefree now. Time changes things, and we all have responsibilities: Dave and Rosie are now engaged, Mel is currently saving for a house, Rosie is just about to start her role as a junior doctor at Romford General Hospital and Si is about to embark on a PhD on the use of mummification during the Egyptian period. Creepy. But at least he is following his interests.

And then there is Martha. They say twins are supposed to be similar in characteristics and personality, but even though we both have wavy blonde hair and blue eyes, and are both five feet seven and three quarters (to be precise), that's where the similarity stops. Martha is more outgoing than I am. If you see a crowd of people, Martha is bound to be at the centre of it. I prefer my own company. Someone has to be the quiet, sensible one. Two crazies together don't equal sanity.

Sadly, despite being the sensible one, I seem to be the drifter, with no idea of what I want to be or do. Martha already has a job lined up in Australia as an IT consultant. I am tagging along in the hope that I will find more to life than watching a photocopier churn out another 100 pages of 'blue sky thinking' or answering the telephone to another imbecile who doesn't know how to switch on a computer. But mostly, I am hoping that this trip will bring me Love.

As 'Land Down Under' by Men at Work starts to blare through the lounge speakers and Martha drags me into the centre of our circle of friends, everybody in the room gets up to dance. Even Granddad Shane has a go, clearly hyperactive after too many lemon sherbets. As I look around the room I realise, not for the first time, that I am so lucky to have these people on my side. Even if they are all weird. I love them and I will miss them, but tomorrow I am going to fly to the other side of the world and a whole new chapter of my life will begin.

CHAPTER 2

Women. I love them. As long as they are naked and don't mention the 'R' or 'B' word. 'R' for Relationship and 'B' for Boyfriend. There are too many women in the world to experience to be tied down to one. I want to be free and have fun.

Miss Wednesday mutters something from under the duvet, something about not being able to find her bra.

'It's under the bed,' I reply, trying to remember if her name is Laura or Lauren or something else entirely. Still, it doesn't really matter. Time for her to leave. Time to kick her out. In a nice way of course - I am not a complete bastard.

'Thanks for a great night Ryan,' says Miss Wednesday, as she slips her boobs into her bra and reaches behind her to do it up at the back. 'We will have to meet up again some time.' Her boobs look very tempting, and she is looking up at me seductively. But her panda eyes from not taking off last night's make-up, and the orange streaks left by the fake tan on the bedsheets bring me back to earth and I mumble: 'Sure we can meet up again. On the 12th of Never'.

'What did you say?' she replies, pulling her dress over her head.

'I said just send me a text and we can meet up whenever.' A good save. Once she has finished dressing I lead her to the door and tell her that I am going to be late for work. She gives a fake pout, and then blows me a kiss as she leaves. I breathe a sigh of relief when the door closes behind her. At least she left before she had the chance to eye me up as her potential Prince Charming as I am anything but. I'm just the King of Toads in the virtual pond of internet dating, where you take your pick, have your fill, and then go back to fish out another to satisfy those mid-week urges.

One woman I definitely won't be hooking up with today is my mother. She has left me a text saying 'Call me'. Most people know of her. She is Doctor Lara Turner, the relationship guru, Australia's answer to Dr. Phil. There's isn't a billboard in sight that isn't emblazoned with her name and details of her talk show and the column in *Cosmopolitan* magazine that gives advice on how to get the love life you deserve.

She first came to fame 12 years ago after divorcing my Dad. She was 43 and wrote a book called 'How to be a Cougar'. *How to entice that youthful man using just a smile and your well-earned wisdom.* Or, as I like to call it, 'how to grow old disgracefully.'

Before the divorce and *that* book she was just an average psychology lecturer at the University of Sydney, as was my Dad, but then she suddenly decided she wanted more from life. She's currently dating a guy a year younger than me. He's called Larry and she is apparently having the best sex of her whole life. These are things a son never wants to hear about from his own mother.

Meanwhile, my Dad took the divorce in his stride. He said that he totally understood mum's desire to follow her own path, and he agreed that he should follow his. And I should follow mine. Sometimes I think spending too much time studying psychology has done their brains no good at all.

Dad is now living in Perth in a permanent state of mid-life crisis. His latest idea is to train as a surf instructor. He is dating a woman who looks like Madge Bishop from *Neighbours*. 'Madge's' current obsession is knitting tea cosies. I have received several. They are decorating the inside of my bin.

So, not difficult to see why I prefer to lead a single life. I'm damaged.

En route to the train station from my apartment in Bondi, with another day of number-crunching in the CBD on Martin's Place ahead of me, I decide to give Mum a call. After three rings she picks up.

'Hi Darling. Mummy wants to know if you'd like to join her and her fluff ball of fun for dinner tonight as it would be lovely to catch up and see how my little boy is growing up.'

I'd rather eat dog food on my own in a broom cupboard than have dinner with 'fluff ball'. Mum on her own I can handle. But with Larry? God, it is just unbearable. Last time I went to dinner with them he insisted on calling me 'son', even though it's not even biologically possible, while continually stroking my Mum's leg. Awkward doesn't even begin to cover it.

I give my excuses to Mum, narrowly avoiding a night of sheer hell with her and her peculiar lover, and then I decide to text Pete to arrange drinks after work tonight. That will ensure a much better night of entertainment and will give me a chance to find my next catch. Miss Thursday.

CHAPTER 3

It is raining. My first ever day in Australia and it is raining. This wasn't what Greg the travel agent told me Australia would be like. Even my own Dad, who was born in Australia, sold me an image of a country where there is continuous warm, sunny, hot weather. I was preparing myself for a place where the sunbeams would warm my back as I sit on one of the many glorious beaches watching equally gloriously tanned lifeguards from behind my oversized sunnies.

Instead, I am soaked through by pounding rain as I struggle up the hill from the train station with my rucksack, which is now broken and has only one strap left. So instead of 'living the dream' and eyeing up some Aussie hotties, I am now hauling my bag across my back as if I am auditioning for a female version of the Hunchback of Notre Dame and hoping this nightmare will end.

Martha is already several paces ahead of me.

'Hey Martha! Can you slow down a little…I'm kind of struggling here.'

Martha swivels around and shouts back; 'Come on Ruby, don't be such a whinge bag we are nearly there.'

Eventually we make it to 'Wally's Hostel' a small little place tucked away on a side street called Woolloomooloo Street. The outside looks kind of grotty and the painted wooden sign on the front saying 'Wally's Hostel: a home away from home' is peeling away. The photo of the smiling woman next to the slogan looks rather jaded and is verging on ironic. But it is tipping it down out here and I am desperate to get inside just to dry off. Besides the inside might be better than the outside.

I had been too optimistic. A strong smell of stale sweat and dust fills our damp lungs. The walls are a sickly yellow, faded that shade, I suspect, from an original white. The wood cladding on the walls and on the front of the reception desk is faded, with those that aren't crying out for a lick of paint just simply missing. In the far corner is a dead eucalyptus tree. The last thing I would say was that this was a home away from home, if my mother saw this place she would have a heart attack as to how unclean it is and everything would be covered in bleach before we could even breathe in the place let alone sleep in it. Greg the travel agent has a lot to answer for.

'Greetings,' says the guy behind the reception area.

'You must be our new guests, Martha and Reuben.'

'It's Ruby not Reuben,' I reply biting the inside of my cheek...

This guy is a bit of a prat. And a creep. He gives me a stinking yellow-toothed grin that makes him almost blend in with the peeling yellow paint. After a moment he slowly licks the bottom of his lips, eyeing me up and down while pushing back his lank long greasy hair.

'Oh I do apologise, for some reason I had the booking down as one female and one male in the 18-bed mixed dorm.'

'No that's incorrect,' Martha says firmly. 'It should be two females sharing in an all-female dorm consisting of eight beds.'

'Well I am ever so sorry about that mistake; let me see if there are two spaces in the all-female dorm.'

He clicks away at the dusty keyboard and squints at the computer at the reception desk.

'Sorry girls,' he says after a few minutes. 'There's only one space left in the female dorm tonight, so one of you will have to go in the mixed dorm.'

Fan-bloody-tastic. It takes me over 24 hours to get here, 18 of which were spent squashed next to an overweight man whose last shower may well have been more than a fortnight ago. And he snored like a rhinoceros for most of the journey. Then when I do finally arrive, I discover at the baggage carousel that the airport luggage handlers had chosen my bag to play football with, and it was now battered and torn with just the one strap, its pissing it down outside and now they haven't even booked us in properly.

Martha turns to me and takes a deep breath.

'Okay, we will have to settle this fair and square…rock, paper, scissors.'

'No Martha, not rock, paper, scissors as you know you always win.'

'Perhaps I can assist?' pipes up Creepy Guy. 'How about I flip a coin?'

Okay this guy is a creep but I will give him credit for his suggestion.

'Okay let's do that, I choose heads and Martha you can have tails.'

Surprisingly Martha just shrugs her shoulders and agrees to it and we await the result of the coin toss.

Creepy guy puts his hand into his grubby blue jeans and pulls out a two dollar coin.

'Okay girls here we go...'

*Please be heads…please be heads…*god why is it taking him so long to flip a bloody coin?

I see the two dollar piece somersault in the air and then it lands with a clink on the brown hairy carpet just beyond the reception desk. He leans his skinny frame across the desk and announces the result.

'Tails.'

Great.

Creepy Guy hands us our keys and then leans over the desk until he is just millimetres away from my face. I think I'm going to vomit.

'Here I can make up for it by letting you have a free packet of crisps from the hostel's food store,' he whispers in my ear.

I snatch them from his hands, but only out of politeness. They are out of date and they aren't even Walkers. What I would do for a packet of Walkers Roast Chicken crisps right now. I've been in the country for no more than a couple of hours and I already miss home comforts. This adventure really isn't what I thought it was going to be.

'Where's the lift?' I ask, hoping that this will be the last conversation I will ever have with Creepy Guy.

'Sorry ladies there is no lift here. Stairs only. I would offer to take them up to your rooms but I hurt my wrist the other day taking the trash out,' he says, shrugging and flashing another grimy grin.

I take a deep breath and head up the five flights of stairs to my dorm room. Martha is on the third floor, and despite her athleticism being much greater than mine, even she was red in the face from hauling her suitcase ever upwards. Still, my rucksack may have broken its strap, but at least it isn't a suitcase on wheels. I think I may have a slight smug smile on my face.

The smugness didn't last long though. I feel like I am going to die. I need some rest. I lean my weight against the door to catch my breath and as I do so the door opens. Suddenly I am face to face with a pair of testicles.

'Hey I'm Andre.' I try to look above the testicles, and just make out a bearded face with enormous spectacles that starts to talk to me.

'Sorry about the lack of clothes but most of them are in the wash and the outfit I had today has a whole load of beer down it from working a busy shift at the local pub. Besides I feel much less inhibited without the clothes.'

I try to play it cool and pretend it's the most natural thing in the world to talk to a man who is stark naked but I have a feeling my bright red face gives it away.

'What's your name by the way?' asks Andre in what sounds like a Welsh accent.

'I'm Ruby.' I offer my hand for him to shake but I am hijacked by the thought that Andre may have touched his genitals just before I entered. And I pray to the Lord I have packed a jumbo bottle of antibacterial hand wash in this rucksack.

'Welcome, Ruby, to the palace. Tonight, as you can see, you will be sleeping in the penthouse suite with 17 other sweaty strangers. How does it feel Ruby to be surrounded by such luxury?' he asks with a big grin.

I want to tell him that is my worst fucking nightmare. Instead I just flashed him a smile.

'I can't wait, I am looking forward to the adventure,' I add. I suspect he is not convinced, and he chuckles.

'Oh an adventure it will be, Ruby. When you find out what sort of animals, both human and non-human live in this place. I will give you a quick run-down as to who's who while it's quiet. You look like a newbie to this hostel lark, so it seems best I give you the heads up on how things run here.'

First of all he points to the far right corner of the room where there are four bunk beds. 'That's a group of Chinese students here to do English. Very peculiar lot they are. I've tried to speak to them a few times and they all start staring at the screens on their phones and pretend they haven't heard me and leave it to one called Ken to answer me back. He's polite enough but he tends to give one word answers, although I swear that Ken isn't his real name.'

'Then you have Laurence, a decent chap from London, aged 27, on a working holiday visa. Having a break from the 9-5 life as a software engineer back home, but out here he works in a bar, it's the same one as me. It's the Juicy Parrot Bar on Kent Street; it's basically a backpacker's bar full of lots of sweaty bodies wanting to get as plastered as quickly as possible. A few local guys also go so they can find themselves a new foreign acquaintance, if you get my drift.'

I immediately cross the Juicy Parrot off my must-see list whilst in Sydney.

Andre then continues with his lowdown of the rest of the inhabitants in the human zoo.

'On the bunk above Laurence is James. He recently turned 21. He is a bit opinionated but that may be the drink talking, he seems to always have a bottle of something in his hand. He's here with his friend Dean; it's rather funny that their names make up the actor James Dean. Shame neither of them share the actor's charm. That's Dean's bed to the right over there.'

I can't really see Dean's bed as there is a big sheet tied from one end of the frame to the other. The sheet looks like it hasn't been washed in weeks, but outside there are several condom packets, some of which are opened, and a couple of empty tins of beer to the side. There's also a magazine with a naked woman on the front, pushing her breasts together with her hands and pouting. No wonder she's clutching her breasts, she must be absolutely freezing.

'You have just laid eyes on the Love Den.'

I look at Andre in sheer disbelief; it looks more like a crack den. Andre just shrugs his shoulders.

'This guy likes to bring back his lady friends. He's spent all the money he earned doing construction work out here on booze and can't afford a private room, so that's his solution. He expects we can't hear the jungle noises he makes.

'Then there is Georgia and Sebastian, the Made in Chelsea extras. They're on their 'gap yah'; probably have a friend called Tarquin…Both like to pretend they are roughing it to show they've been on a proper Australian adventure, but they're only here for one more day and then they're off to join their friend

Rupert at his villa in Bali.'

'Next to the Chelsea crew is Pam and Lucy who are basically the female equivalent of James and Dean…so you can imagine what they are like.' He paused for a second. "Actually Ruby, I will have to make an apology as I tend to make judgements rather quickly. You might love all of these people and think I am the crazy one. Especially as I am the one not wearing any clothes.'

We both laugh. Even though Andre is butt naked, I have a feeling he probably is the more sensible one in this room.

'You'll get used to them soon enough though. How long are you staying here?'

'Well I'm hoping to be here for a year, although only in this hole, err I mean hostel, for a couple of weeks. Then hopefully I'll move into a shared house with my sister Martha who's travelled with me….'

'Woah woah,' says Andre. 'No need to give me your life story right now, the basics will do. There's plenty of time to find out about each other as the days go by,' he winks.

'Anyway, changing the topic - looks like you have the remaining bed, number 18, the best bunk of them all.' Andre was grinning.

'Oh really?' I ask quizzically.

'Yep it's the bunk below me. How lucky is that?' At this stage I am not sure whether this is a blessing or a curse. Andre seems sweet enough despite the lack of clothes but you can never be sure about how crazy some people are. I put my rucksack in the locker beside my bunk and begin to survey the rest of the room again. Suddenly the dorm room's door bursts open and a loud bellowing female voice fills the room.

'Oh my fucking god…who does this guy think he fucking is? Seriously, it was nothing more than a one night stand. He needs to get over himself. Actually babes do you know where the nearest sexual health clinic is? I think I might have chlamydia.'

Wow. This girl clearly likes to make an entrance.

'Arrrgghhhh, Andre put some fucking clothes on you weirdo, no one wants to see you with your cock out.'

Andre laughs.

'Hi Pam, how are you? Do you want me to give you a hug?'

'No I don't you freak, just put some bloody clothes on.'

Whilst Andre looks through his tattered bag for some underwear, Pam swivels her head in my direction. She looks me up and down and then a black hole fills the room as she opens her mouth to talk at me.

'And I guess you must be another one of Dean's cast offs. Let me tell you now Missy we are fed up of Dean thinking he can bring any old girl in here to satisfy his needs…'

'No,' I interrupt sheepishly. 'My name is Ruby and I just got here. I'm hoping to spend a few months out here on a working holiday visa to travel the country and have an adventure…'

'Fantastic,' she grinned enthusiastically; though I knew she had lost interest after the point I told her I was new. She clearly had other plans on her mind…such as getting pissed.

'I love it when a newcomer arrives, a great excuse for a messy night. Wheeeeey, let's get on the beers Ruby.'

She pulls out a six pack of beer from underneath her bed and passes me a can. This is not how I wanted my first evening in

Australia to be. I would rather go to bed and get an early night so I can spend a day ticking off all the touristy things I want to do before starting the search for work and proper accommodation. I really didn't want to spend it with Party Pam.

Don't get me wrong I do like a nice alcoholic beverage in a sophisticated bar or at home on a quiet evening in watching a film or reading a book, but when it comes to downing litres of the stuff I am just not interested nor have the liver capacity. My Dad and Martha, on the other hand, can drink like a fish. But the 'let's get drunk and party like a mad man' gene skipped me. I seem to have gained the 'old before my time gene' instead, which is pretty useless when dealing with the likes of Pam.

I slowly sip the beer she handed to me out of politeness and she gives me a hearty slap on the back as if I am some sort of Jolly Roger about to sail the high seas with Captain Drink A Lot. I'd rather walk the plank. But as I try to look for the perfect place to get rid of my can I am backed into the corner of the room by Pam and there is no escape.

'Let me round up the rest of the bitches staying here and we can head to the local backpackers bar.'

'That sounds awesome,' I reply as I plaster a false smile across my face and watch her stagger out of the room. I try to look on the bright side. Tonight could be the night I meet a guy who just got roped in by his friends to attend this 'backpackers bar' and we could escape together and sit in a wine bar and listen to some soul records and talk for hours on end. Now that sounds like pure bliss.

I am rudely awakened from this lovely dream by the returning sound of a fog horn or as she is most commonly known, Pam.

'So, I have rounded up the party bitches and also another newbie. In fact, she really looks like you. Let me introduce you to them before we head over to Juicy Parrot.'

Oh god not that place.

Three scantily dressed girls and one familiar face, all holding some sort of cheap beer, enter the room. The fog horn starts again.

'Okay, so here is Lucy, she has been my best friend since Primary School and we decided to go on holiday together…'

Lucy appears to have been 'on the beers' already as she decides to interrupt Pam's introductions to tell us about Pam's love life.

'Pam also has a massive crush on Dean….'

'Shut up Lucy. Just because you want to get in his mate James's pants doesn't mean I want to get with Dean.'

I really do not care about who wants to sleep with whom, but can see that this is an indicator of the tone of the night ahead of us. Pam then introduces me to Ellie and Vicky. Vacant is the best description of them both. Utterly and totally vacant. Pam then looks at Martha but I can tell she has already forgotten my sister's name.

'And this is…,'

'Martha,' I interject.

'Do you know each other already?' Pam replies slightly open mouthed.

'Yes, she is my twin sister.'

'Shut the front door,' squeals Pam. 'Oh my god, you are twins. That is so freakin' cuuuuuute!'.

Martha rolls her eyes at me. Glad to see my sister and I are on the same wavelength on thinking Pam is a bit of a joke. I sidle up to Martha and whisper in her ear.

'Please get me out of this.'

'Not a chance,' she grins back. 'You need to stop being so boring and enjoy a bit of party time to celebrate our arrival in Oz.'

I had a feeling that was going to be her answer, but it was worth a try. It's off to Juicy Parrot's we go then. Although I feel sick rather than juicy as a parrot already after having two cans of this cheap beer.

Before leaving the hostel for hell on earth this evening, I grab my floral tea dress from my broken bag and put it on in the dorm's pathetic excuse for a bathroom. I then slick on my favourite red lipstick, brush my hair so I look fairly presentable and give a wave to Andre who is now wearing some pants.

He mouths to me 'good luck'. I think I am going to need it. I follow the other girls out of the hostel and into the now dry and warm night air. I really hope that this is all part of the journey to find love.

CHAPTER 4

5:25pm. Just 5 more minutes until freedom and the end of this god awful meeting with Bert, the guy from pensions with the permanently coffee-stained tie. He screams middle management, with his briefcase and endless PowerPoints on "blue sky thinking". He is currently trying to convince me and my fellow accountant colleagues the importance of reminding our clients to have a pension when dealing with their business accounts. As if I don't have enough to do already in ensuring their books are balanced and they aren't going to go into liquidation.

Other than the crazy ass clients I occasionally have to deal with such, as Mrs. Morell and her pet Chihuahua who likes to slobber all over my shoes; I actually love my job. The guys I work with in the office are pretty solid and provide some serious banter.

People always thought I would go into psychology and follow in my parents' footsteps. There was no way I was going to do that. I know how loopy that has made them. In accountancy, there is no craziness, no emotion. It is just all about the numbers. That's how I like things.

I catch Pete's eye and make a yawning gesture followed by a drink of an invisible beer, he responds back with a nod and a thumbs up. I can always rely on Pete to spend a night on the town whatever the day of the week; he is almost as bad as me, although I may add he isn't quite as good looking or as popular with the ladies as I am.

Finally, Bert has decided that we are in enough of a corpse-like state to bring the presentation to an end and just as he says 'thank you for....' I have already pulled the metal handle on the glass door of the meeting room in order to get a step closer to freedom and soaking up a room scented with beer and pussy.

Just as I leave I feel a hard slap between my shoulders.

'What's the rush Turnstile? I thought you'd want to stay and get Bert's autograph after that outstanding performance.'

I turn around and see it's just Pete.

The nickname Turnstile was coined by him as it's a play on my surname Turner. For some reason he finds this name hilarious and has managed to convince all my other friends that this should now be my name, although unfortunately for him his surname is Higginbottom so you can imagine the fun I had with that one.

'Na you're alright Piggy, I saw you sniffing round him and didn't want to get in the way of your budding romance there.'

'So...' says Pete, putting all six foot three of him tall and wide in front of me and ignoring my brilliant comeback. '...I think the plan for tonight should be dinner and beers at the Hudson and then once we are suitably lubricated we can head to Juicy Parrot to see what's on their menu tonight. Wink. Wink.'

Ah, Juicy Parrot, how I love that place. It's the perfect place to pick up some desperate backpacker who is looking for the chance to be swept off her feet by some rugged Aussie. And I know just the person to make that happen. I agree with Pete's plan.

'Excellent,' replies Pete, who then decides to unbutton another button on his pink striped shirt, showing off a huge pile of chest hair that could probably keep a small family of four warm for the next month.

'Mate what are you doing?'

'We are going out.'

He is looking at me as if I am the one who's decided to release the beast sitting on my chest.

'Yeah I know but I didn't realise you were treating me to a strip tease before we leave the office.'

'Ha-ha mate, I wouldn't do that as you might get jealous over this sexy body…'

He begins to make rubbing motions up and down his body as we walk down the stairs out of the office and I start to think whether I made the right decision to go out with Pete tonight. In this mood he might seriously hinder my chances of finding Miss Thursday.

Thankfully he stops rubbing himself all over and concentrates on getting out of the building through the sliding glass doors as quickly as possible. Thank Christ it was just us in the stair well at that point and no one in the office saw that display. As much as I like to have a laugh and party I do like to maintain my professionalism in the work place. I am good at my job and I don't want anyone to have any reason to take me down from being the top of my game as a high-ranking accountant at

Charter & Charter.

Pete on the other hand is a bit on the lazy side and focuses more on the social side of the office rather than the work side, but manages to do just enough to prevent himself from being in the firing line.

Just as I think I am safe from any more of Pete's outbursts, as we walk towards the Hudson he begins to explain further to me why he was giving his chest some air.

'Tonight is party night and as its party night you need to undo the third button. Or as I like to call it the 'party button' so everyone knows you are up for one HELLUVA Party! Woohoo!'

The loud boom of his voice startles the elderly Chinese man walking at a measured pace in front of us, so much so that he stops and looks at Pete in shock and amusement. This then encourages Pete to up his 'party mode' even further by singing at the top of his lungs the Black Eyed Peas 'I Gotta Feeling'.

'TONIGHTS GOING TO BE A GOOD NIGHT…'

This bloke hasn't even had a drink yet and he's acting like a loon. I'm hoping some decent Thai food at the Hudson will calm him down a bit otherwise I am going to have to find a way to ditch him.

Pete grins at me, knowing he is making me uncomfortable. I am starting to get a little bit pissed, and not in a good way.

'Pete mate, you're getting a bit too loud so I'm going to start walking ten paces behind you now as you're starting to cramp my style'.

'Sorry Turnstile, it's being stuck in that office all day, it gives me cabin fever. I will calm it down now. Besides I am more starvin' than Marvin.'

Luckily just as I am on the verge of punching Pete in the face we make it to the Hudson, and the waitress clearly knows what Pete's appetite is like and points him straight to the buffet bar. I have never seen a man pile so much food on one plate so quickly. Some of us are more dignified and take time to muse over what's on offer. Plus my slow approach to the buffet bar gives me a chance to eye up the pert ass of the petite brunette waitress as she struggles to open up a bottle of wine for a dining couple.

In between hoovering up his meal and downing several beers, Pete manages to drone on about work. I'm not sure what's worse - Party Pete or "please help me with my accounts exam" Pete. That's typical accountant stuff for you. We tend to be obsessed with our work and given any opportunity we will bring it up, and if we don't bring it up its probably because we are too busy studying the subject, hence the reputation accountants have of being all about work, work, work. And not in the sexy Rihanna kind of way.

However, despite working hard I still find time to party hard and it's time to cut the chat about balancing figures and start looking at some hourglass figures in Juicy's instead as the choice at Hudson is rather slim, especially as the brunette I was eyeing was flashing her wedding ring. The simple suggestion that we should now head off to Juicy Parrot brings back Pete's party mode.

'YES MATE! LET'S GO AND FIND SOME SEXY FEMALES'.

And this is exactly why Pete has trouble pulling girls.

When we arrive at the bar it's already heaving and there isn't as much eye candy as I had hoped. As we wait to be served our next drink I begin to think of who in my list could be available for a booty call and to cut my losses. There's Michelle, one of the company receptionists on the floor below although I heard she's now dating a banker called Doug. There's Stacey, but she works nights at a bar now. And Tanya. Yes, Tanya looks like the best option. I send her a flirty text. Instantly she replies.

Miss Thursday is in the bag.

Just as we manage to get some drinks, Pete spots his cousin Craig at the other side of the bar and we head over to meet him. From the looks of Craig's t-shirt ('I'm trying to give up sexual innuendos but it is hard…so hard'), I can see the pulling women thing is something of a family trait.

'Yo Turnstile,' yells Craig. 'It's good to see ya. How's it going? It's been a busy week with me solving everyone's IT problems…' Having just managed to shut out Pete's work woes, I'm really not up for listening to his cousin's problems too.

Luckily, we are all distracted by a group of girls making a loud entrance into the bar. The ring leader looks totally wasted, the slightly chubby ginger girl clinging to her arm is continually shouting her name, Pam, and appears to be as equally as drunk as she is. She also seems to have pulled up her skirt so high everyone in the club now knows the colour of her knickers.

Behind the two mouthpieces are the rest of their group and they all head straight to the now very crowded bar. Two of them in the group look very similar in appearance, although despite the similarity, one of them stands out more than the rest of the group.

It is almost as if she has stepped out of an enchanted garden with her wavy blonde hair, skin like bone china, full red lips and eyes a deep midnight blue. As I take a moment to absorb the image of this unusual girl in the floral dress, I notice that Craig has already stomped his way over there and is already making a fool of himself. The girl looks rather repulsed, and after a few seconds of conversation between the pair, it is clear Craig has missed the mark. Craig tries to coolly swagger back over to us and then shouts: 'I THINK SHE'S A LESBIAN!'

Craig is clearly not one for admitting he sucks at getting a girl, neither is he one for realising how loud he shouts. The girl must have heard what he said. She starts to come closer and looks like she is going to lose her shit with Craig. Trying to stifle my laugh I decide to back away to avoid getting involved.

As I turn around to make my exit from the situation I am confronted by a pair of tits and I recognise them instantly. It's Tanya.

CHAPTER 5

Pam has no shame. She is currently dry humping a wooden pillar at the side of the bar we've all just walked into. There's not even any music playing in the background. Seriously she needs to stop acting like such an idiot and retain some of her dignity. And doesn't she know that she is at risk of getting splinters up and down her legs from the wood?

This is the third place we have visited this evening and each place seems to have gotten grottier and grottier. We haven't even got to Juicy Parrot yet. The guy behind the bar here has enough piercings in his face to start his own scrap metal company and the decor wouldn't look out of a place in a 1970s horror movie.

I am sitting on a beer stained brown leather sofa, squashed between Martha, who somehow seems to be enjoying this evening, and Lucy who is lining up her next strawpedo. Despite being squashed like a sardine, I try to maintain a lady-like composure and sip my glass of white wine as the other two in our group, Ellie and Vicky, sit on the arms looking at themselves on their phones for the umpteenth time.

After staggering from her make shift podium, Pam stands right in front of us as if she was auditioning for X Factor, puts her hands on her hips and starts her fog horn impression again;

'Right I think we are all suitably smashed so it's time to head to….'

She leaves a pause and I am keeping all my fingers and toes crossed in the hope that she has finally tanked up to the max and wants to go back to the hostel.

'BURRRRRRRRP….' Just when I think she couldn't lower her standards any further she decides to release the most noxious gas in all our faces. Please god tell me what I have done wrong to end up on a night out with this animal.

'OOOH DEAR ME…well on that note lets head to JUICY PARROT! Wooohoooo!' bellows Pam.

Shoot me now.

After a five minute walk and queuing outside for what seemed like an eternity we finally got into the questionable place that is Juicy Parrot. It lived up to all my expectations. Loud boisterous backpackers and sticky floors.

As Pam and Lucy make another spectacular entrance I do my best to distance myself from them and so does Martha. We head to the other end of the bar and get a drink there. As I wait for another glass of wine, praying that my liver can take it, I see that Martha has already caught the eye of a girl wearing a plain low-cut black dress with straight black hair, black rimmed glasses and red lips. She stands out from the crowd, quite tall and with biceps that make Madonna look like she hasn't worked hard enough at the gym. She walks towards us and introduces herself in a beautiful Spanish accent;

'Hi, my name is Chloe. What brings you both to Juicy Parrot?'

Despite her addressing this question to the both of us, it is quite clear that she only wants to talk to Martha. And Martha clearly knows she wants to talk only to her, as she begins to move closer to Chloe. As they get deeper and deeper into their conversation I get pushed further and further to the side lines taking on the usual role of third wheel. Martha has clearly pulled. This is when I start wishing for a handsome man to come along and whisk me off my feet.

'My names Craig' shouts a big fat sweaty guy, so close to my face that I get my own personal spit shower from him across my cheek. This guy isn't handsome, he is horrific.

'Hello…I'm Ruby,' I respond, pulling out my best British accent, aware that this guy was looking for any female mouth to stick his tongue in. As he touches my arm I feel the hairs on the back of my neck rising. I just want this leech to go as far away as possible from me. His beer-soaked breath is hot and heavy on my cheek as he says:

'You have pretty eyeballs. Of course they'd be better if they were eyeing my pretty balls.'

I swipe his sweaty hand from my arm and venomously hiss at him; 'Get off me you scumbag! That is not a way to speak to any woman.'

His hamster-like cheeks begin to turn a pinkish colour from embarrassment, and then in a desperate attempt to save face he turns away to shout across at his friends.

'I THINK SHE'S A LESBIAN!'

Martha and Chloe must've clocked what had happened as they are holding down my arms in order to prevent me giving this guy what for, for the rude and ignorant comment he just made. It's then that I notice his friend who is trying to stop himself laughing over what has just happened. He looks confident and self-assured. His hair is brown, he's tall at around six foot and he has broad shoulders. He is wearing an expensive tailored navy suit and white shirt which makes him seem older, but I guess he is probably roughly the same age as me, in his late twenties. I can tell from his divine green eyes that he is a total and utter charmer. I am not sure whether I should be falling in love with this guy or telling him he is an absolute arsehole.

As my rage over the incident begins to subside and I take in the lout's friend in a bit more detail, I feel a sudden release from my arm as Chloe removes her acrylic nails that had become almost embedded in my skin as she tried to restrain me.

'Don't bother with that pig, he is just proof that evolution can go in reverse,' she whispered, and I laugh out loud, turning away from Craig and his friends. But I can't stop myself from wanting to look back again at Craig's well-dressed friend. As I turn, I see that his eyes focused on the chest of Pamela Anderson's cute Asian counterpart who is wearing a plunging teal dress cut so low I wonder if she has it on back to front.

I've decided. He's an arsehole.

After what feels like an eternity pretending to enjoy the latest pop drivel pumping out of the stereo, the sound system finally shuts down indicating its closing time, which is perfect timing for Pam as she is being dragged out by her hair by the security guy after leaving her Technicolor mark all over the guy's shoes.

Just as we step out of Juicy Parrot's I see Craig sucking the life out of some poor girl. He has clearly met his match. Her t-shirt is emblazoned with the words 'I love my lady humps'. I am glad I avoided that sleaze and I am glad that at 4am in the morning we are finally heading back to the hostel.

As the more sober one of the group I am given the task of dragging the remains of Pam across the pavement to the hostel, and as she is such a good friend of mine now I make every effort to ensure her lumpy body feels every part of the Sydney pavements on our journey back.

When we finally arrive, I commit the ultimate sin by just going to bed with my make-up and clothes on. Not even my Mum's nagging voice in the back of my head is enough to pull me from this hostel bed and stop me falling asleep.

*   *   *

After what feels like ten minutes of sleep, streaks of light flutter across my eyelids and I realise it's no use attempting to lie in. I can hear all sorts of weird noises - people shuffling and talking in different languages. As I fully open my eyes in readiness for the next day of strangeness in a foreign country I am greeted by the large brown eyes and scruffy mop hairdo of Andre who has popped his head over the bunk.

'So how was the first night out in the bright lights of Sydney?'

'Horrendous,' I reply.

'Looks like you won't be spending much time hanging out with Party Pam then?'

'I'd rather eat my own eyeballs than spend another evening with her.'

I suddenly realise I may have said that too loud and she may have heard, but as I look over to her bunk I see that she is still in a comatose state and probably won't be awake until sometime this afternoon.

Andre then swings down from his bunk and crouches down to

my bunk;

'I've only got a short morning shift today as I am doing the clean-up shift at the bar and I wondered if you fancied walking around the city a bit with me. Just to clarify this isn't a date or anything, you're a nice girl and all but you just aren't my type. I hope I haven't offended you…I'm not saying you are ugly or anything…in fact you are quite pretty…just I don't have that attraction to you….'

'Andre…please stop talking…you are digging yourself a hole, yes I'd be keen and don't worry despite seeing you naked I have no attraction to you either.'

'Ah okay…glad we've cleared things up. I'll meet you outside the front entrance at 3pm then?'

'Sure, see you then Andre, I'll make sure to stand a couple of steps behind you so people won't think I'm your girlfriend.'

Andre looks back at me slightly open mouthed and then after seeing the smile on my face realises I am joking and lets out a small chuckle which sounds as if a small toddler has been tickled with a feather.

As he leaves the dorm, I think about everything that went on last night and let the realisation that I have actually left the UK and made it to Australia sink in. The first evening may not have gone to plan, but there are plenty more days to come, plenty more days to fully enjoy this country. Oh god, I need to stop thinking about things as it is making my head pound, which is probably due to the fact that I drank my bodyweight in alcohol last night. I get up out of my bunk in the search of a glass of water to help my hangover and as I do so I see a blonde bombshell sitting up in the bunk opposite me.

CHAPTER 6

I tug at her peroxide blonde hair as I push my tongue further into her mouth as she lies on my black silk bedsheets ready to get and give some satisfaction. I want it fast and I want it physical.

Her dress is already strewn over my bedside table and my shirt and trousers are a crumpled mess on the floor. It's time to get down to business and make this Thursday a night of delight.

She's already gagging for it; she is wet and ready as soon as I put my fingers inside her. Sometimes it is just too easy with Tanya: one phone call and she's already on the verge of coming.

The foreplay doesn't last long as I slip on a condom and enter her and begin to rock back and forth with pleasure. I watch her mouth round in an o-shape and push deeper and deeper until I hit that ecstatic moment of climax.

As I break myself away from her, she looks at me breathless with a starry gaze in her eyes and whispers 'Well that was fun!'

'Glad you enjoyed it,' I wink back at her as I edge slightly away from her across the bed. The first time she slept with me she snuggled up to me post-coitus and I immediately wanted to throw her across the room. I do not do after-care. I don't need cuddles. Plus, I am not her boyfriend. If a girl wants a boyfriend they need to look elsewhere. I want and enjoy the bachelor life.

After the first 'hug-gate', where I wrenched her slender yet solid arms from my chest; I laid down the rules with Tanya and told her straight that we are just friends, albeit friends with benefits, and if she wanted to snuggle up to someone either she needed to find another guy to do that with or she needed to get herself a teddy bear.

That doesn't stop her getting ideas in her head though. Sometimes she thinks that she might be the one girl who can change this playboy into a respectable and monogamous loving man. When she starts the talk of 'have you ever thought about having a girlfriend', I immediately shut her up by giving her a mouthful of kisses. It works every time and before she knows it; it's time for round two.

I met Tanya through GirlmeetsBoy… god how I love that app. It is basically sex on tap. You just keep swiping and typing until you get a girl is who ready and waiting for you to take her clothes off her and show her a good time. Although there is a catch.

There can be girls on that app who look like total babes in their picture and would definitely score an 8 or 9. When you meet them in real life it's a different story - they look more like a Babe of the pig variety, and if that's the case I usually summon up a fictitious sick Uncle and scarper home to put the fishing rod back into the online dating pool and hope for a better catch.

Tanya matched her picture, right down to the same tight-fitting fluorescent pink strappy dress and six inch black stilettos. We had a drink at Buoys Bar by Darling Harbour, followed by quite few more drinks and then…well you can guess the rest.

Tanya seems to love the fact that I am a few years older than her. She told me that what attracts her to me is my self-confidence and my good job in the city. She seems to forget to mention though that I am also dynamite in the sack: maybe she wanted to spare my blushes when telling me how much of a stallion I am. I can be such an arrogant fucker.

Luckily, she has never asked what I like about her as I don't think the answer of great tits and a compliant pussy would be the compliments she was looking for.

Image over substance is important to Tanya when it comes to friends and boyfriends. This is clearly evidenced by the fact that she refuses to go anywhere without having a suitable amount of bronzer on and a tonne of mascara on her face and that any guy who approaches her without a suit or any girl who hasn't decided to raid the whole Crayola collection and put it on their face is a 'bogan'.

Tanya once said that I remind her of Clarke Kent but without the glasses: I can't remember how much alcohol she consumed before she told me this but it must have been a lot. I think secretly she hopes that I think she is Lois Lane. Maybe I could introduce this as some sort of role play. The thought of this is starting to make my ticker lively again and I wonder whether Tanya is still awake and up for another root.

As I turn over in the bed to see whether she is as horny as I am I see that she is already flat on her back in a deep sleep and taking in large gasps of air. This is one of the downsides of having Tanya as a fuck buddy; despite her deluded sense of reality as to how she thinks men should be, she snores like a rhinoceros in heat. It's not ladylike in the slightest.

As I watch her cause a small earthquake in my flat I wonder whether I should recommend one of Mum's psychology books to her, just to point out that I am the bad example and the guy you should avoid, not the good example that may appear mischievous but is actually an angel underneath. However, I am enjoying the random sex too much to burst her bubble just yet.

Occasionally I pity her for pinning her hopes on the fact that one day she will change my ways, so I take her out to a nice restaurant for dinner rather than inviting her back to mine. Besides it's nice to have some eye candy to look at while munching on some steak rather than having to look at Pete from work dribbling all over the place and adding another gravy stain to his shirt.

After a long day of work and play I feel my eyes begin to shut ready for the adventures of tomorrow, already preparing for kicking Tanya out in the morning. It can be exhausting entertaining the women of the world, so I decide that I will let this week's potential Miss Friday enjoy life a little longer without meeting the wonderful Ryan.

I think it is time to chill out with the boys after work instead. Besides it's important to put the bros before the hos anyway.

CHAPTER 7

I wipe my eyes again to make sure I am not still asleep and to check that the rather handsome chap with the beautiful blonde hair in the bunk opposite is real and not a figment of my imagination. I look down at my hands and see that I have black marks on the back of them.

Shit…I really should have taken my make- up off. Now I am going to look like a panda that has been dragged through a hedge backwards. Unless, since the 24 hour plane journey here and last night, the latest fashion embraces the local bag lady look I am not going to make the best first impression on the blonde bombshell.

As I look back from my stained hands and up to his top bunk I see that he is beginning to get changed, grabbing clothes from his backpack at the end of the bed. I sit up a little, thankful that I have the bunk with the prime view of his strip tease.

And the vest is off…ding dong. This guy has a body to die for. He must have sensed that I was watching him as he turns the back of his blond head along with his gloriously tanned and toned body towards where I am sitting, mesmerised.

Avert the eyes Ruby…avert the eyes…you do not want to be known as the pervert in this hostel.

It's too late; he catches me looking and gives me a small smile. I smile back and instantly realise I probably look like a demented loon with my black eyes, last night's clothes and a cheesy grin. As he begins to change into his pants and shorts underneath the duvet, I decide to get myself into gear and find myself my make-up wipes and a t-shirt and shorts to change into. And as if someone just loves making my life a real life sketch show, the first t-shirt I pull out has a picture of a panda on it.

As I fumble through my bag for a more suitable t-shirt I feel a shadow get closer and closer to me. Then the most richest and beautiful English accent fills my ears…

'Hey I'm Laurence'

I turn to face the talking shadow and see it is the blonde bombshell. He is inches away from me, and as I take in the full beauty of his six foot four muscular body and beautiful face with kissable lips, strong but well carried Roman nose and heart-melting delicious brown eyes, I attempt to respond to his greeting.

'I'm Rrrruby,' I stutter back.

For god's sake, I need to get a grip and prevent making myself an absolute idiot of myself in front of this real life Adonis.

'Nice to meet you Ruby,' he smiles.

'How long are you here for?' I ask without the stutter this time.

I really hope that he is here for the same time as me and that he is a newbie too and…okay I'm getting too excited and just need to calm down. I look intently at his pretty face and wait for his response.

'Well I've been in Australia for almost eight months now. I started off travelling the east coast and then settled in Sydney where I've worked in the bar down the road for six months. I had my last shift there two nights ago. The place is called Juicy Parrot, absolute shithole but the pay there was good. Now me and Carmen are off to a random town in Western Australia to do a couple of months farm work.'

As soon as he mentioned a girl's name all the glorious fantasies of Laurence and I holding hands on the beach, dining out in fancy restaurants together, going to funky and kitsch art galleries and choosing names for our future children are shattered in an instant.

Who the hell is Carmen? Why do I want to kill her already and why is this guy already leaving? And why oh why do I always get attracted to the men that are unattainable?

'I'm due to meet Carmen and her boss in about an hour or so: it's her last day. She works in the florists inside Martin Place Station. I think you'd like her.'

Hahaha yeah right Laurence, I'm sure I will totally love a girl who got her claws into you first.

'I am sure she is lovely and what a cool job to be a florist,' I reply, hoping it doesn't come across as too obviously sarcastic.

He rubs the back of his tanned neck and begins to gaze at the floor. Clearly my bag lady look was even worse than I thought and he can no longer look me in the eyes, or at what I have on.

He then speaks to the floor and says to it; 'Do you fancy coming with me? We can grab some breakfast on the way as it looks like you've had quite a hard night of partying and it will give me a chance to find out what brings you to Australia.'

I double check that it is me he is speaking to and that he isn't asking the carpet or anyone else in the room to come with him, and respond with a positive 'yes please.' I sound like the team leader of The Desperado gang. Yet Laurence suddenly straightens up and takes his hands from his pockets, smiles and then pauses for what feels like eternity.

Oh god…maybe he was just asking out of politeness and now he is trying to find a way out of spending time in Sydney with the bag lady from Britain.

He then breaks the silence and replies in a loud voice;

'Awesome. I'll see you in reception in about ten minutes to give you time to change, unless of course this is how you normally dress for the day?'

I am not sure whether he is joking or not but I am too busy already planning my outfit for breakfast to give a detailed response so I give a small smile and tell him I will be down in ten minutes.

Thirty minutes later, I make an appearance dressed in my black shift dress and my painted floral Doc Marten boots. Smart but casual. Perfect for a breakfast date. I apologise for my lateness but Laurence doesn't seem to mind. We walk to the nearest café which is clearly pastry heaven. All the food in the café window looks divine.

As we sit and I begin to stuff myself with glorious pastries that are baked to perfection, I find out that Laurence and I have a lot in common. We both live in Essex, we both are sick of working in an office and we both like contemporary art and reading Marvel comics.

Just as I am enjoying being in my own little bubble and getting over my hangover with the beautiful blonde, I hear a ping from his shorts' pocket and he pulls out his phone.

'It's Carmen. I'd better go otherwise it's going to be a painful evening getting to Western Australia. You should come: you might be able to take over her job. Tess, the owner of the place, is looking for a replacement.'

The thorn in my side has returned again. Just as things were going so well.

I begrudgingly agree to go with him despite the fact I do not want to be 'Carmen's replacement', or even meet her knowing she has already snagged this beauty. However, the chance to spend more time with Laurence and the fact I really need to earn some money out here especially as I have probably already blown a few dollars on a pile of pastries means I suck it up and see it as part of the adventure.

Laurence must've read my mind about the pastries though as he pays for us both without me having a chance to say otherwise. Such a gentleman. But unfortunately for me he is a gentleman with a girlfriend.

We walk towards Martin Place station and I begin to wonder just how far away Carmen works if we need to get a train to see her. As we walk down the station steps, there in front of me is a small shop looking like the Hanging Gardens of Babylon, decorating an otherwise grey industrial train station entrance.

As we get nearer and nearer to the floral paradise, I spot two women. The first is an older woman, about five foot two with dark blonde curly hair pinned up into a scruffy bun. She has slightly squinty grey eyes and rosy cheeks which match the shade of the tulips hanging in a bucket above her head. She has a bright green apron on with the words 'Fascinating Florals' written on it in swirly white writing. Her jeans have soil stains on them and her black t-shirt underneath is faintly marked with pollen. A true picture of her craft.

The second woman I presume is Carmen. She is at the other end of the flower stall watering the deep purple hydrangeas. She is gorgeous and looks like something out of a Victoria's Secret catalogue. Her skin is a beautiful caramel colour and her green eyes made you melt into a puddle. If I had a huge girl crush on her, then I knew that her proximity to any male would leave them totally under her spell. Any chance I had with Lawrence was blown out of the water. Ugly Betty vs. Naomi Campbell. And we all know who would be better at punching if it came to a fight.

They both immediately spot Laurence and come over to give him a hug and giggle together. I feel like the elephant in the room as they exchange pleasantries, and I stand staring at my Doc Martens, hoping I am the modern day Dorothy with her slippers and can click my boots together and go somewhere else.

It doesn't work. I'm still here. And I've just heard my name being said out loud.

'This is my friend Ruby; I just met her at the hostel I was staying at. Ruby is looking for a job. Tess, is there any chance you could take her on?'

Wow. This is the first time a guy has put me forward for a job and the more time I spend with him the more I want to run away into the sunset with him.

Tess looks me up and down.

'So what do you say Ruby…you up for the challenge of selling flowers to the commuters of Sydney?' she says in her gravelly Australian voice.

I suddenly wake up out of my Laurence Love dream, and make sure to pay full attention to Tess as I so desperately need this job. God…boys can be so distracting sometimes…

'Yes of course, I'd love to…'

'You say that now doll, but wait 'til you have to deal with the blokes who begrudge spending fifteen dollars on a bunch of flowers for their missus… I feel sorry for the poor cows having to deal with tight grumps like that.'

She suddenly pauses for a moment, and then carries on her speech.

'Well you look like a good kid and I love your shoes. Plus you Pommies are always a good laugh so I think you and me will get on a treat.' She then points to the delectable Carmen who is the high-end caramel shortcake to my flat and cheap muffin.

'This lady here is leaving tomorrow with this fella as she needs to spend some time with some sheep and get quality time with her man, so I'll need a replacement anyway.'

Carmen laughs. 'Here,' she takes off her green apron and places it over my head. 'I now crown you the next assistant of Fascinating Florals.'

I smile at her sweetly, though my eyes are shooting daggers at her. Tess interrupts my murderous thoughts by asking if I can start on Monday. As she says this she diverts her milky grey eyes from Carmen and me back to her roses, where she gently caresses them as if they were a delicate Persian cat.

'Yes sure,' I reply, hoping that I make no sudden outbursts or display any peculiar behaviour which could take away this opportunity.

'It's an early start,' continues Tess. 'You need to be at the front of the station for 5am to unload the stock and get ready to sell the wares at 6am to the early rise traders and commuters. I will pay you $20 an hour and expect you to work 36 hours a week. You still in?'

5am. Jeez Ruby, you don't half like to give yourself a challenge, do you?

'Yes. I'm still in.'

'Good,' she replies firmly.

There's no turning back now. I've said yes and I will finally get to earn some Aussie dollars. I can't believe how easy it was to get the job and wonder whether there is some sort of catch to this despite the early morning start. It has also sparked my creative juices. Seeing all these flowers makes me want to get my sketchbook out and draw the roses with a deep red hue, the sunflowers with a large brown middle and strong green stem. I pray that my treasured drawing materials are not damaged in my bag and I can rekindle my passion as an illustrator again.

I look back at Tess and push my shoulders back to show I have got this and give her a broad smile in the hope I can get on with Tess and really make a good impression. She gives a small smile back.

'Don't be late kiddo. I'm counting on you,' she says before disappearing behind a group of bonsai trees.

Suddenly I hear Carmen's voice commanding Laurence and I feel my shoulders slump down slightly.

'Laurence, I hope you are all packed and ready to go for 7pm tonight. Don't forget you are meeting me here to get the train to the airport. Also, could you get me some cherry ripe for the journey and also some tim tams?'

'For God's sake Carmen give it a rest, I have never been late, and as for the snacks get your own. I've spent enough dollars on you this trip feeding your addiction.'

He then looks at me as if to say it's time to go, so I say my goodbyes to both Carmen and Tess and then I turn and walk with Laurence, with a feeling of slight satisfaction that he put Carmen in her place.

As we walk up the steps from the station to the city, he turns and says to me;

'Do you think me and Carmen look alike?'

What a bizarre question to ask, why would a guy want to know whether his girlfriend looks like him?

'Ummmm I don't think so, I wasn't really paying much attention to whether you both look alike,' I lie to him, knowing that I took in every inch of their glorious bodies.

'Ah right, well people say we both have some similar features, not surprising though considering she's my step-sister.'

I am pretty sure he just said that Carmen is his step-sister.

'My step-sister has been living in a flat in the Northern Beaches with a guy,' he continues.

'I don't really like him; I think he is a creep. In fact he is the reason that we are off to the middle of nowhere. If she does her farm work she can get an extra year on her visa so they have more time to then get a partner visa. I think she is making a big mistake.'

I honestly couldn't care whether Carmen ran away to the circus and married a clown as long as she is related to him it means I still have a chance with him. Suddenly he stops and touches the side of my arm and I feel my face flush a deep crimson.

'Sorry, I have been talking a lot about myself. Changing the subject slightly, I'm just meeting my friend from the bar I've been working at to say goodbye before I head off tomorrow night. If you want you can come along too…unless of course you are getting bored of my company?'

Following this delightful invitation, he gives me the cutest grin ever and I just literally want to throw my arms around him and kiss those full beautiful lips. I so desperately want to spend time with this guy. I want to know more and see if he will bring me closer to the love I crave.

I suddenly remember I am due to meet Andre in about an hour and know I will have to decline the invitation. It's the unwritten Ruby rule. Ever since Mel, my supposed best friend at university, decided to ditch me and leave me on my own for my twenty-first birthday to go on a date with a guy she just met two days before and who cheated on her two weeks after, I have made sure that mates are always before dates. So since then it has always been mates before dates. Although I am hating myself right now for making up that rule and even though I have known Andre just under 48 hours I just know it would be wrong to bail on him.

'Really sorry Laurence, I said I would meet up with Andre from the hostel this afternoon. Although could we swap numbers or something as it would be great to stay in touch.'

There is another one of Laurence's long pauses and he seems a little taken aback by my response.

'Sure, that's the first time a girl has asked for my number. Normally it's the other way around. Here type it into my phone.'

Great, I've come on way too keen and he is probably going to take my number now to be polite only to delete it later. Clearly misread the signs on this one.

'Thanks Ruby, I'll text you later. I'd like to stay in touch.'

Yeah right, and the Queen likes to send me a telegram each week. I'm not expecting to hear from this guy again after my forward behaviour.

Suddenly he kisses me on the cheek, says goodbye and turns away towards the warming sun and I feel similar warmth in my stomach, although my throat feels dry as a sense of disappointment and lost opportunity forces me to swallow hard.

I hope Andre is going to pull something awesome out of the bag this afternoon to make this sacrifice worthwhile. Also, it had better involve copious amounts of chocolate as I need something to lift my mood right now.

*   *   *

I stand for a moment in silence taking in the magnificent view and feel lucky that I get to see the image of the beautiful white sails and grey rainbow in person rather than on a postcard or TV. Sydney Harbour Bridge really is beautiful.

Andre rudely interrupts my day-dream.

'It's a bit overrated for my liking. At the end of the day it's only a bridge and a slightly odd looking building. I'm not sure what all the fuss is about. These people should come to Wales and spend some time in the Valleys, now the views you get there really are, something to talk about. Come on let's go to Luna Park and have a go on some of the rides. It's only a quick ferry ride away and a much more fun view than this one.'

I'm half listening to what Andre is saying and half day-dreaming about what me and Laurence would be up to if we both were walking round the harbour, admiring the view, visiting the MCA and organising a trip to the Opera in the evening. Such lovely images in my head.

'What is up with you Ruby? You seem a bit distant. And I know it isn't because of me as I am such a superb person to hang around with,' he says jokingly.

'Sorry Andre, I was just reflecting on the nice time I had this morning with Laurence.'

'Pfffft. You don't want to chase after Laurence; he is off and out the picture. Besides, I think he is quite boring. All he used to talk about was cooking, tech and contemporary art.'

I open my mouth to respond but he places a finger over my open lips to stop me.

'Sssh child… I don't want you to start defending the man, he's done and dusted. It's time to get you out dating missy, see what the land of plenty has to offer you. Have you been using GirlmeetsBoy much since you landed?'

I look at him completely baffled.

'You don't know what GirlmeetsBoy is do you Ruby?' he grins mischievously.

I look at him still puzzled and now mightily embarrassed. It feels like the time when I was little and I thought a tampon was a different breed of tadpole. To this day my sister still teases me about it.

Andre then begins to wave his hands in the air in front of me as if he is about to perform a magic trick;

'Let me introduce you to a world of many men at the swipe of a button. One swipe and you could be galloping off with Prince Charming. Or at least having a quickie with his slightly weird brother.'

I look at him still confused by the whole thing and wondering why I would want to date Prince Charming's weird brother.

Andre then lays out his right palm in front of me.

'Right give me your phone, you have Facebook don't you?'

'Yes, I am not that much of a philistine Andre.'

I obligingly hand him my phone, intrigued as to how many single men could be sitting and waiting for me in this magical virtual world, and why I hadn't heard of this app earlier. A few seconds and taps later, I am now a fully-fledged member of GirlmeetsBoy and Andre is already swiping through men to find me a match.

'So we have a Mark aged 29… no he looks a bit of a knob, okay next is… Tim aged 23 likes to cycle and also has a picture with what looks like a pet dog. Ugh, it's a poodle. So that's a no and a swipe left for him, next is…'

'Give the phone here Andre, if I am to go on a date with one of these men I would like to choose who it is and not go on a date with a complete nut job.'

'Oh sorry Ruby, I can get a bit carried away on GirlmeetsBoy, in fact one night I swiped and responded to so many girls I ended up with four dates all on a Tuesday evening.'

I am shocked as to how much of a lothario Andre was because of this app. I mean, no offence to the guy, he is a good friend to hang around with but he has this slight 'dweeb' vibe about him, partly due to the thick framed glasses, brown messy hair with a fringe that he is constantly pushing to the side so he can see, and a body that is too skinny and long and usually, if isn't walking around naked, is decorated in superhero t-shirts and black cut off shorts. As cruel as it sounds, if there is hope for Andre then there has to be hope for me.

Andre hands me back the phone and a tingle of excitement runs down the back of my neck and my heart starts to beat slightly faster. I cannot wait to see who is out there and whether they will match with me.

First up is a guy called Gareth aged 32. An immediate no. He is a full on Goth with black lipstick and eyeliner. He looks depressed and is wearing more make-up than me. Right who's next?

'Errgh this guy looks gross,' I say to Andre.

Andre is literally breathing down my neck like a psychopath, so I might as well share the screen and fulfil his interest in seeing who I match up with.

'I agree,' he replies. Those five seconds of Ricky, aged 30, wearing a mankini that does nothing to cover the gorilla hair that covers the rest of his body can never be erased from our minds.

Up next is Danny, aged 26. Cute. Dimple on his cheek and thick curly dark hair. Swipe yes.

'Look you've got a reply from Danny already,' Andre shouts scaring half the passengers queuing on the harbour for the Luna Park ferry, and making it obvious to them that I am on a man-date hunt. If my face gets any redder today I may stay permanently looking like a tomato.

I read the message aloud to Andre.

'Are you a Middle Eastern Dictator?'

'No…are you sure you were meant to send this question to a girl on a dating app?' I type back to him.

He responds within seconds.

'…because there is a political uprising in my pants.'

I leave the conversation there with a feeling of disgust. I hope that joining GirlmeetsBoy isn't going to be a complete waste of my time.

Then a Ryan aged 27 pops up on the app. I swear I have seen him before. He is dressed in a smart navy suit and in one of the pictures he is holding a small Labrador puppy. That's a clever ploy, but I can't help but fall for it and swipe right. He replies instantly.

'Hey gorgeous :)'

'Wow, he thinks I am gorgeous.' This is a much better start than Disgusting Danny.

Okay time for me to play it cool.

'Hey Ryan, how are you?'

'I am good thanks. U?

Okay this guy thinks it is okay to use just a letter instead of the full word which smacks of laziness and a lack of grammatical skills but I'll give him a chance just because he called me gorgeous.

A few more messages exchanged and suddenly I am going on a date tomorrow with Ryan at a bar called Luciana's. I look at my phone in slight disbelief. In the space of five minutes I have snagged myself a date. The last time I tried to get a date I ended up spending forty-five minutes talking to a Where's Wally lookalike in a library, only to discover he had a vegan girlfriend who liked watching weird YouTube cat videos. I sometimes wonder whether I am the weirdo in situations like. Maybe this will all change in Sydney. I've already spent the day with the blonde bombshell and hopefully will have an exquisite evening with Ryan tomorrow.

Andre's welsh accent fills my ears again;

'Are you alright Ruby, you look a bit shocked. Are you not a fan of ferry's or amusement parks? We can go somewhere else if this doesn't float your boat. Excuse the pun.'

I look up at him and whisper to him: "I've got a date Andre. I've been here only five minutes and I have a date."

'Calm down Ruby, it's only a date and I am sure it will be the first of many in this city. Now let's get on this boat and head over to Luna Park where I can bash you into oblivion on the dodgem cars.'

'Yeah right Andre, clearly you have not heard of my reputation as Ruby the Racer, you'll be the one needing to dodge not me.' I grin and then look one more time at the GirlmeetsBoy app and the picture of Ryan cuddling the Labrador.

The Australian adventure of love may have just begun.

CHAPTER 8

Buzzzzzzzzzzz. I make sure to hold the buzzer for at least a minute on my arrival at Chad's apartment on Lamrock Avenue, Bondi. The buzzer is basically his alarm clock, even though it is Friday night. I've never known someone to sleep as much as Chad and it isn't as if his life is stressful.

Even though Chad is completely different to me, he is the yin to my yang. The Bert to my Ernie. If there is one guy I trust completely with my life it's him.

I met Chad at the local swimming club when I was 12 and he was 15. He had just moved to North Bondi from Cronulla and was immediately labelled as the 'weird Shire kid'. As my father hailed from the Shire I didn't see why being from South Sydney was such a problem. Although some kids in North Bondi can be right snobs.

To be honest he did come across a little bit weird to begin with. He would just introduce himself to everyone and talk about everything under the sun to anybody who was in talking distance. He didn't care if it was the most popular girl in school, the swim coach, or the pool janitor, Chad did not discriminate and would do his upmost to be friendly to everyone, even if they were a douche bag in return.

At the time I wasn't the most popular of kids. I'm not really sure why, but I seemed to be a prime target for the swimming club bullies. I loved the actual swimming at swim club and relished just shutting off the whole world by pounding out a few lengths in the pool. I won a few medals as well, which was nice. The bit I dreaded would be changing before and after the swim session. Every time I was heckled, whipped with a towel, my swimming trunks were stolen and chucked in a hard to reach corner, or my dry clothes slung into the pool.

The ringleader was a kid about twice the size of me. He had a mean mouth and mean punch, which meant the other boys went along with him, afraid they would be the next victim. He was nicknamed the 'Raging Ranga' due to his fiery temper and bright ginger hair, although no one called him that to his face.

I just accepted the punishment with the hope that it would eventually stop. It did stop. Not because the Raging Ranga had given up but because the weird Shire kid who did not give a flying fuck about his image and whether he was popular or not told the Raging Ranga and his mates to go do one and stop picking on me.

At the time the Raging Ranga was furious that Chad had challenged his authority and attempted to engage Chad in a fight. Little did he know Chad could administer the most brutal of Chinese burns and Raging Ranga screamed like a girl when he was on the receiving end of one, and this made me howl with laughter.

He was humiliated and left the changing room with his oafish mates without uttering another word. As soon as they left Chad then began to chat to me about what ice cream he was going to have later, as if the incident had never happened. And from that point onwards Chad, the slightly odd shire kid became my best friend.

He has always been what I would call a stereotypical surfer dude. You know the type. He has shoulder-length blonde hair, a permanent tan and bright blue eyes which are enough to make any girl throw off her bikini. He also has a tendency to end every other sentence with 'Dude' and if he gets any more laid back about life he would be horizontal.

He currently rents this apartment in Bondi with his long-term girlfriend Charlie and another flat mate called Dave who is just plain weird. I once caught him eating sardines from a tin which he had covered in yoghurt. Like I said just plain weird.

I always feel like I am still a nineteen year old student at Chad's apartment. The bin always seems to be overflowing with a variety of takeaway boxes, cleaning is a low priority and the wall is covered in random surf posters or marks of an undistinguished nature.

Charlie claims none of the takeaway boxes are hers as she is on a vegetarian, gluten-free, no sugar and low GI diet. Basically the "lets only eat the food that looks like cardboard diet." Although I bet when Chad's out she stuffs herself with a fully loaded meat pizza and loves it. The dirty slut.

Most men nearing the age of 30 might think it would be time to let the student life go, maybe grow up and aim for a nice clean place of your own with no dodgy décor. But Chad doesn't give a monkey's. I can imagine at the age of fifty that his place will still be the same and that he will still be living here with Charlie and some other random he met on a beach somewhere. Fingers crossed, I hope the random doesn't have any weird fish habits like Dave.

I can however, just about tolerate Dave but when it comes to Charlie, that's a whole different kettle of fish, as she is one of the most pretentious and up-her own arse women I have ever met.

Chad eventually buzzes me in but as I open the door I am immediately confronted by Miss 'up her own arse'. She looks me up and down as I walk through the door. She's not really one to judge considering she looks like a down and out Danni Minogue. If she actually made an effort and wore some make-up she would be much more attractive.

As always she offers me a warm greeting;

'Well, if it isn't the lothario of Sydney. Sorry love, there aren't any girls with their legs open here, you need to go elsewhere.'

'Oh Charlotte, why don't you take yourself and your stupid harem pants that make you like you're wearing a diaper and piss off, I'm here to see Chad not you.'

She hates it when I call her Charlotte, but she was totally asking for a mouthful of venom back.

'Just do one Ryan, I sometimes wonder how you and Chad are even friends, especially with your attitude of feeling the need to sleep with every attractive female you clap eyes on.'

I get ready for a good come back line for her before she disappears back to her bedroom but it's too late as Chad the UN Peacekeeper arrives on the scene.

'Duuuuuudddeeeeee. What's up with you and Charlie man? As soon as you two are together there is just a really negative vibe, it's not good, that's how you end up a constipated and grumpy old man before you hit 30.'

'Yeah well…' God I sound like such a teenager but I feel I need to justify myself, especially against that bitch.

'…Charlie is making me out as if I'm some sort of gigolo when all I want to do is have fun with women who want to have fun too.'

Chad rolls his eyes.

'Well Dude maybe Charlie has a point, chasing after all these girls has got to be exhausting, besides don't you want to find that one special girl who can look after you and share both the good and the bad times with, just like me and Charlie do.'

I give him a look of 'don't talk such bullshit' accompanied by a one-fingered salute.

'Don't give me that Ryan; you know secretly Charlie and I are right. Look let me get in the shower and freshen up and we can hang out at the Beach Hotel for a bit. Don't tell Charlie but I am gagging for a chicken parmigiana. And it can be hard to get that meat fix in without her noticing and having a mini meltdown.'

I laugh in response and nod to show acceptance of Chad's plan and then head to the flat's dingy living room where I see Dave sitting in the corner wearing a cat suit onesie watching Sponge Bob Squarepants.

He looks in my direction and throws me a 'Hey Dude'.

I just nod my head and hope that this is the only conversation I have to make with Dave as I'm not sure I can cope with dealing with such a nut job.

As I try to make myself comfortable at the other end of the room, balancing my buttocks on the faded velvet green sofa so as not to end up being swallowed down the middle, I decide to occupy my time with my favourite hobby - searching GirlmeetsBoy for the next batch of hotties.

Let's see whether one of them would like the honour of being my date.

Okay first up on my screen is Georgia and she is just odd with a capital O. Her face looks like something out of Finding Nemo. She's all big rubber lips and bulgy eyes. Her skin is orange and her hair is full of stringy brown extensions. I don't think even RuPaul would want her for his drag team.

Next is Sophie. She looks hot. Not quite sure about the lip piercing but she has a hot brown bob and sexy green eyes and in some of the photos she is showing off her moves on the pole. Boy, can she use a pole. She looks fun. Swipe right. Instant response. She's keen.

'Hey Babes if you want fun times then call this premium rate number 0800 123 456 for sexy chat to real life sexy chicks,'

Damn. I thought I was getting good at spotting the bots on this app. Oh well on to the next one.

Ruby, aged twenty six. Cute, beautiful blue eyes, wavy blonde hair and wearing a bright red cardigan. Wait. I swear I have seen her before in a club or something. Actually, she looks like that chick who gave Craig hell the other night. Clearly not a lesbian.

She stands out from the rest of the GirlmeetsBoy crowd. She is one of the few people who has actually put photos up without using a filter or pouting as if her life depended on it and isn't pushing her tits to make them bigger than what they are. Clearly a newbie to this. Swipe right. Let's see if we can get her closer to laying in my bedsheets.

I'll begin with my classic 'Hey gorgeous' line and see whether she will grab the bait.

Oh yes. Thirty seconds and she has responded. This is going to be easier than I thought.

Okay she's now asking questions about me. I immediately suss her out as a girl who is looking to get to know a guy and see whether she can relate on some deep emotional level shit or something. I go along with it and tell her what I do for a living, I'm an accountant, I love swimming and surfing, travelling and meeting new people blah blah blah. I continue the act for a few minutes and then go in for the kill, asking her for a drink at Luciana's.

An immediate yes. Boom. Date for Saturday sorted.

'Dude, time to go.' Chad arrives freshly scrubbed wearing his ludicrously bright tropical short sleeve shirt and camel coloured shorts.

'Winner, winner, chicken dinner,' he says loudly rubbing his hands together.

 'Chad,' pipes Charlie from another room. 'You better not be eating meat. Remember meat is murder.'

'Oh shit, I didn't think she would hear. Let's go Dude, before I get quarantined.'

We make a swift exit and I close the app on my phone and I put my phone back in my shirt. I'm feeling smug that I have another girl lined up for some down and dirty on the weekend.

CHAPTER 9

It's Saturday and as I walk back into the hostel with Andre after another pastry-filled breakfast, even the smell of rising damp and old sweat that greets us as we walk up to our dorm can't ruin my mood. I have a date tonight.

I head up to the dorm room with Andre and I see Martha standing outside and spot immediately she is going to tell me something I really don't want to hear. And then I see Chloe, from the other night at the Juicy Parrot, cowering behind my sister despite the show of muscle. My mood begins to sour.

'Hey sis.' Martha is trying the big-eyed-innocent look, and is clearly trying to soften whatever blow is about to follow. There is a long pause, and Martha starts to draw imaginary circles on the floor with her shoe.

'Christ Martha. Just spit it out.' you have that look on your face and as your twin sister I know what you're about to say is bad news so just spit it out.'

When she finally speaks, her voice begins to crackle.

'Well, you know Chloe…'

'Yes Martha, I do. She is standing right behind you. I am not blind.'

'…well we are kind of seeing each other now.'

'Well I kind of figured that out Martha, although I feel there is more news to come.'

She takes a deep breath.

'There is more news. Chloe has a spare ticket to see Dolly Parton tonight and asked if I would like to go with her. I know you love Dolly and we've spent our childhood prancing around to Jolene on Mum's record player… but would you mind if I went with Chloe?'

I'm wondering how long I can make her feel guilty, knowing that I already have plans for Saturday evening. Plans that I would never change, even for Dolly. And then Andre spills the beans.

'I wouldn't worry about it Martha, Ruby has got a date later tonight anyway.'

I could kill Andre for ruining my fun, but my face is too full of embarrassment for me to do anything about it.

Martha grins and looks like she is about to tease me, and then thinks better of it. She can't be sure I won't cause her grief about Dolly and ruin her date night with Chloe.

Chloe slowly appears from behind my sister and begins talking at 100 one miles per hour.

'Can I help you get ready and stuff? I'm actually a make-up artist, I could make up your face, if you don't mind, plus it will be good to know a little bit more about Martha through you, seeing as you are her twin sister…'

I take a moment to absorb the train of words Chloe has delivered and then nod in agreement for the sake of an easy life. And besides, it might help my chances this evening. I also know it will wind Martha up.

We all go into my dorm room and pull out the make-up I have, which by the looks on Chloe's face is clearly not enough. I also pull out three dresses I could wear this evening. I ask the girls and Andre to help me make my choices. Voices fly in my ears from different directions.

'Go for the red, you'll make an entrance and he will notice you immediately.'

'No too powerful, you want the flowery dress you wore out the last night.'

'Don't wear that, you'll look like an old granny. Go for the black wrap dress, it has a hint of practicality but also playfulness.'

This is getting way too complicated and I feel like stamping and saying I will go in my t-shirt and jeans and be done with it all.

As we look intently at my bed deciding which outfit to choose, the dorm room swings open.

'HELLO GIRLS…so what's going on here then…?'

Oh great. Party Pam is back and it looks like she has had a couple of beers already.

'Hi Pam, I'm not a girl but I will say hello back to you anyway.'

Good. Andre is dealing with the situation and hopefully he can tell her to bugger off.

'The girls are busy preparing Ruby for her date. She needs help in choosing a dress which must be   fun but not overtly sexual.'

I am going to make Andre a pot which says on the side 'I owe Ruby $10 for every time I drop her in it'. I think I will make quite a lot of money from it.

Pam snorts and makes a sound like a pig ready to be fed. Then she makes her way closer to the bed where my dresses are laid out. I hold my breath and hope to god she doesn't spew on them, laugh at them or both. Her jaw drops open and the room vibrates;

'I am well good at choosing outfits to get dates. I've got quite a good pulling rate. There isn't much choice here; you should really get your flesh out otherwise no man is going to want to fill your stocking if you get my drift. Go for the red dress and wear it back to front to show off your cleavage that should be the winner. Anyways enough of the chat babes I've gotta go…I'm off to the next door dorm as Dean and his friends are having a Goon night which means I am going to get totally and utterly WASTED! Woohoo!'

And with a hiccup and stumble over a few of the suitcases in the room she makes her exit.

Thank Christ for that, and as for the red dress I'm definitely not wearing it if Pam likes it – it just screams slut rather than sophisticate. And as for what a 'Goon night' is? I dread to think.

I decide on the black wrap dress and black heeled sandals with my gold St. Christopher pendant and gold bracelet. Chloe then sits me down in the middle of the dorm and places all my make-up beside me, and adds some of her own from her handbag. Like an artist painting a picture, she begins to measure up my face using a blusher brush and then gets to work on making me more Coco Chanel than Coco the Clown.

'Ya esta!'

'Pardon?' I respond, taken slightly aback thinking Chloe has made a complete mess of my face or she has suddenly noticed a huge spot that no amount of make -up can cover.

'Ah sorry, I have a tendency to slip back into my native Spanish when I get excited. It means 'that is all'. Your transformation is complete.'

'Wow!' exclaims Andre. 'Ruby you are looking good, if your date doesn't find you attractive after all the effort you've put in tonight then he will need to get his eyes checked!'

I look at myself in the dorm's speckled bathroom mirror and for a few moments I feel like a confident and pretty 26 year old who is ready to take on the world and find The One. Maybe this is it; maybe this new start in Australia was what I needed to find love. I calm myself down and tell myself not to get my hopes up too high. I make my way to the dorm door to leave as its 7 already and I need enough time to get to the bar.

I tell the others I need to go and in unison that all say 'Good Luck'. The butterflies are going crazy but I have a good feeling about this date.

Before I leave the room I glance up at Laurence's bunk. Instead of a blonde bombshell looking at me I see a dirty old man, probably a tramp, who has scraped up enough dollars to stay the night. He makes a wolf whistle sound and then begins to scratch himself all over. Gross. I leave and hope that my bed won't be covered in fleas by the time I get back tonight.

*   *   *

I arrive at Luciana's dead on 7:30pm and wonder whether I have found the right place. In my head I imagined Luciana's to be this small speakeasy bar with a cosmopolitan edge to it rather than a 'cheap and cheerful place' full of suspect men and scantily dressed women. I check google maps on my phone and it definitely says I have arrived at my destination.

At the front of the entrance is a woman wearing a Hawaiian grass skirt and bikini top with a big badge attached saying 'Hi I'm Hayley, Welcome to Luciana's'.

I go up to Hayley and ask whether a table or space at the bar has been reserved by a Ryan Turner or whether he has arrived and is expecting me.

She purses her frosted glossy lips together, looks me up and down before saying: 'Are you for real, who do you think I am Psychic Susan?'

Who does this girl think she is? I'm on edge as it is and I do not need this lip from a bad hostess dressed as a hula girl.

'Well, Hayley, last time I checked I don't think I entered the Matrix. So, yes, I am real and this is not my virtual counterpart. And with regard to whether or not you look like Psychic Susan,' I paused to look her up and down. 'Much more Slutty Susan, I think. Don't you?'

A full on cat-fight is only just prevented by the arrival of an attractive male with an Australian accent.

'Hi I'm Ryan. By the looks of things, Hayley, I think you may have met my date for this evening. I am a friend of the manager; he normally keeps a VIP section for his friends.'

He produces a small white card which has the words 'Luciana's Exclusive Members' embossed in silver and some writing in a blue fountain pen on the back. Hayley takes the card, and hands it back to him, smiling sweetly. She clearly fancies this guy. And clearly wants to hang on to her job.

'Sure thing Ryan, it will be my pleasure to show you both to the VIP area,' she rolls her the 'r' sound around in her mouth, hoping to grab Ryan's attention and be as be as seductive as possible. Back off Hawaiian Barbie, this one is mine for the evening. As she shows us to our table and gives us both a copy of the drinks menu, she makes sure to serve mine with daggers and his with an eyeful of tits.

My heart feels like it is pounding out of my chest. I have never felt so nervous on a first date. Mind you that may be because most of the guys I've previously been on dates with have the 'I've just got out of bed' vibe to them rather than the 'I'm super hot' vibe.

Play it cool Ruby, play it cool. Even the way Ryan sits suggests a man with an air of confidence about him. As he reads the menu I take the opportunity to take him in. The slight wave in his thick brown hair neatly frames his face and shows off his square jaw and emerald green eyes, and the light blue shirt shows off a figure that is suitably toned. As I look at his feet I see he is wearing smartly polished brown Italian leather brogues. It's always a good sign when a man has well-kept shoes.

He can clearly feel me watching him and he slowly licks the top of his lips before he locks his eyes with mine. Nerves get the better of me and I start talking.

'I've never been a VIP anything, so thank you for having me as your VIP guest this evening.'

'You're welcome Ruby. I do the accounts for the manager who runs this place. I work as an accountant at Charter and Charter and we get a variety of clients, and sometimes they come with perks.'

He pauses, gives a cheeky grin to Hayley, who is deliberately hovering over our table, and orders us some cosmopolitans. He then continues with the conversation.

'Being a VIP at places like this is a bit like having your virginity taken, all that anticipation and excitement and then at the end of it all you just feel like there should be something more to this.'

Woah, where did that comment come from, you have just met me and decide to make some weird comment about virginity. I let the comment slide and wonder whether it is because he is nervous, though his bravado stance of sitting up straight and looking me dead in the eye suggests otherwise.

'So Ruby, tell me a bit about yourself. I am intrigued to know what lies behind those gorgeous blue eyes of yours.'

'Well as you may have already guessed I am British. I am actually here with my twin sister, her name is Martha'

'Oooh twins, now you are talking Rubes, any chance of a threesome then?'

He then laughs a rather dirty laugh and awaits my reaction. I really wish he would stop making such stupid comments. It makes him sound like some sex-obsessed weirdo. I'm going to see if I can get to the bottom of this and see if I can find the real Ryan rather than the randy Ryan.

'Seeing as you have asked me a question Ryan, let me ask you one.'

He seems to be taken aback slightly by my assertiveness and for a moment I have a brief feeling of satisfaction that I am now the one in control on this date.

'What's your most vivid childhood memory?'

Now this guy is definitely on the ropes. He is just staring at me as if I have just asked him to work out the square root of 57869 in under three seconds, although for some reason I think he might be more comfortable in answering a maths question then something personal.

He clears his throat. It looks like this guy will not be defeated by a challenge and this immediately makes me like him again.

'It was when I won the 400 metres butterfly stroke at the local swimming gala when I was 12. I remember seeing my friend Chad and my parents jumping up and down in the stands, cheering me on as I smashed through the water. Seeing them supporting me gave me that extra push to make sure I won. I remember the looks of absolute joy on their faces when I collected my gold medal. I should get back into my swimming a bit more really.'

I smile on the inside, gleeful that I am actually starting to get under his skin and find out more about him. I try another question to see how far I can push this.

'What's something you are really proud of lately?'

'Wow, you are good at asking some rather intriguing questions! Do you know what Ruby I am going to have to pass on that one as I can't think of one off the top of my head.'

Now he is starting to melt my heart. He has a look of a lost boy. I know I have hit him deep. It looks like I have got through his barrier of being the wannabe womaniser and can start connecting with him.

'What's something you always wanted to try?'

'Well Ruby, I kind of hinted earlier, I really want a threesome. Any chance your sister is free tonight?'

For Christ's sake, just as I thought I was getting somewhere. I decide to ignore it and fire him another question.

'What's the last book that you read?'

'It was the Karma Sutra. Nah, only joking. It was actually Advanced Accounting for the Working Practitioner. If you haven't already realised, being an Accountant is a pretty big deal'.

As I sip on my fourth Cosmopolitan of the night, I continue with the questions and try not to be shocked at some of the sexually laced answers. I find it difficult to make up my mind about Ryan. Usually during a date, I think the guy is either a potential "no-go" or a potential "let's go and run away together" and this guy has dipped in and out of each category throughout this evening. So far in this date there have been times where we have had deep meaningful conversations about music, cinema or art and then other times he seemed to feel the need to chuck in some inappropriate lewd comment.

They do say opposites attract though so maybe this is the guy I'm looking for or maybe I'm just drunk and desperate and clinging on to any hope that this date has potential to blossom into a relationship.

My head is beginning to spin.

Ryan leans in close to me. He whispers in my ear that he loves my British accent and the dress I am wearing this evening. The tension between us suddenly becomes intense and I find that the only way to relieve it is to take the plunge and kiss him.

His lips feel soft and warm against mine and...woah, he's moved in with the tongue already. Okay time to break away and take a breather for a moment. That was fast. As I take in the intensity of the kiss he begins to stroke the back of my arm and he whispers in my ear again.

'So how about we carry this on at the hotel I have booked this evening.'

Wow, this guy definitely thought he had this in the bag before he even met me.

'Why do you have a hotel booked?' I say trying to act inquisitive when I feel slightly peeved he thinks I am an easy catch.

'Well on the walk to the hotel I will tell you the reason why.'

I look at him not sure whether to kick him, laugh or be impressed by the way he is trying to seduce me. And for some reason despite my head being filled with alarm bells screaming at me that this guy just wants to use me for sex I still feel the urge to go with him.

Do you know what? Fuck it. You only live once. I'm in Australia and the world is my oyster, and why shouldn't I just have fun and have sex with this guy? So, some of his jokes are really jarring and he is clearly a bit of a playboy. I might not get the chance of such good looking male company again…oh god I really think I have had had too many cosmopolitans…

Despite the doubt in my mind I grab my purse, which remained shut thanks to Ryan's act of chivalry in paying the bill, and I kiss him passionately one more time before we begin to head towards the hotel. I keep my fingers crossed that this act of spontaneity will lead to something special.

CHAPTER 10

Blue shirt and chinos. The standard Ryan pulling gear. It's always best to keep colours plain and neutral as it stops the girl being distracted and focuses her on my face where I can use my eyes to focus on her to emit confidence. Then I add a smile to show I am friendly which puts a girl at ease. It is one of the few useful things I picked up from my parents' psychology lessons.

A spritz of aftershave and I am ready to go and hit the city and head to my date. I even have a hotel booked. My mother was given a free room at the Sydney Skyscraper Hotel as the manager their loves her books. She was due to go there tonight but she can't make it so she has asked management to put it in my name. One of the few perks I get of being Dr Lara Turner's son.

She can't make it as her and lover boy are off to Adelaide for some last-minute radio talk show she's agreed to do to tell women that it's okay to be a cougar.

It really isn't okay to be a cougar though. These women should be called another c-word. Cradle snatchers. It might stop them looking like a desperate loved up idiot and it would save their sons and daughters being subjected to some jumped up dweeb the same age as you wanting to be your step-father.

Being able to have a hotel room to bring a girl back to is often much better than bringing her to mine as it makes me more mysterious and I know girls totally dig that James Bond vibe. I do my best Sean Connery impression in the mirror and I think I sound pretty good, I might try it out on Ruby, what with her being a Pommie and all. I'm sure she'll love the James Bond routine. Surprisingly, out of all the women I have rooted, I have yet to get a Pommie so I am rather hyped in finally getting to tick doing one off my list.

Before heading out of the door I do a bit of research on my phone as to what gets Pommie girls going. From the looks of things, they love a bit of 'cheeky banter'. I don't really know what that means so I will just go with the normal Ryan Turner charm as it has a pretty high success rate with all the other girls I have dated.

Right, time for one last check of the mirror, a flex of the 'guns' and I am ready to meet Ruby and give her the night of her life.

As I arrive at Luciana's I notice Ruby immediately at the entrance. She looks even more stunning than her GirlmeetsBoy pictures. I can't wait to see her naked. Her blonde wavy hair looks almost golden and the black dress she is wearing hugs her in all the right places.

Unfortunately, her pretty face is starting to get all screwed up as she is clearly pissed at the girl manning the entrance. I wonder whether to let them fight it out and spy on some girl on girl action. I decide to intervene. A fight between two women would be fun, but not as much as having one of them all to myself in a bedroom ripping my clothes off.

As I wave my VIP card for Luciana's, Ruby turns and gives me the most beautiful look with her blue eyes. She looks truly impressed and slightly in awe that I have VIP access which is rather sweet as most of the other girls I have been on a date with see this as standard fare and would be rather hacked off if they didn't get the VIP treatment. All I can think is that Ruby must have been out with a lot of 'Budget Barry's' in her time. That's a shame. She would suit dinner at the Shangri-La rather than at Macca's.

This can play to my advantage though.

Although women are about as hard to read as a book written in Martian, so there is no guarantee that she will want to hook up later. So just in case things don't work out with a girl I meet online I always like to have a backup plan. And tonight the backup is Hayley the hula girl.

I try and play the two off of each other. First I work on the hula girl by looking her up and down and smiling as she hands me the cocktail menu. I was tempted to give her a little wink but I feel Ruby's eyes on me and decided not to push my luck.

I then sit square on to Ruby and look directly into her eyes and show off my confidence. She looks at me and then looks away knowing that her eyes give away the truth. She already finds me attractive.

I keep quiet and flit my eyes between Ruby and the cocktail menu. I'm going to let her sweat it out and make her take the first move and I can then build on it from there. It's a standard Ryan trick.

As I wait for her to crack I count the seconds in my head. Six seconds. Clearly she does not like awkward silences. Excellent, I have found a weakness I can use to my advantage and I can already take control of the situation.

She asks me a question about how I managed to get VIP status. And despite me going for the whole cool vibe I ended up blurting out the most mundane response to her question.

Wow. Ryan can you hear yourself? You sound like such a pussy going on about your accountant job. Remember to flirt not divert. The more time you talk about yourself the less time you have to make your intentions clear.

I follow up with a killer line to bring the topic back to sex and she looks unimpressed. I feel a bit embarrassed. I've cracked out jokes like that before and not thought much of it, and some girls literally snort out their drinks at some of the sex jokes I've told so I am not sure why I feel awkward saying stuff like this in front of this girl.

Keep cool Ryan. You are just warming up and clearly this Ice Queen in front of you needs more of your sexy charm before she melts into your arms.

I decide to ask her about herself. Girls love to talk about themselves. As she begins telling me her life history it gives me time to admire the cupids bow above her lips. Before I enter into a daydream state that usually helps pass the time when girls start talking to themselves, remaining just aware enough to nod in the right places, I hear Ruby mention a twin sister. And bam. Back in with another sex joke. The threesome. Now I'll know for sure if she's up for playing tonight. If she isn't, then I'll start hitting on Hayley.

Ruby dismisses my threesome comment and then throws me a question so left field I have never heard it on a date before. Turns out that this is too interesting for me to give up on just yet, and I am actually enjoying the challenge of keeping up with her intellect and answering her without giving too much away.

She's high risk though. No guarantee I will be fucking her

tonight. But I find that I am willing to take the risk. And it is refreshing talking about my life for a change rather than feigning interest in someone else's.

I decide to lean over and whisper a compliment, giving me the chance to lift myself off my seat and sort out the wedgie I seem to have acquired this evening. As I move in closer I inhale a lungful of her scent and she smells incredible. And those lips of hers are just pursed to perfection. And suddenly they are on mine. I wasn't expecting that.

Boy, she is a good kisser; let's see whether we can take this further. I push my tongue into her mouth but she pulls away. Looks like it was a bit too soon, but I am sure she enjoyed it so I hedge my bets and suggest we take this action it to the hotel room.

She looks a bit peeved. She asks why I would have a hotel room. Other girls would have jumped at the chance of a night in a hotel, but this one is different. Maybe it's because she's a Pommie. I try a suave swerve of an answer, but I can tell she doesn't buy it. I am disappointed, expecting rejection. But then her mouth defies her and she says yes.

I call the waitress over to pay for our drinks. She's not quite as eager to serve me now she can see I've pulled. But I don't care. Her breath stinks. I've just missed out on an evening with Halitosis Hayley.

As Ruby picks up her purse, I do my best to pat down my trousers and control the semi I have right now so I can save it for the hotel and get fully blown. I'm keeping my fingers crossed that his girl is going to be good fun and that we are going to have one hell of an evening before I say adios and we go our separate ways.

CHAPTER 11

As we walk towards the hotel I take in the scenery and 'live in the moment'. My sister has been telling me for years to stop being so wound up and go with the flow and just enjoy life. So here I am. Going with the flow. Enjoying life. Just walking along the pavement, breathing in the Sydney air, admiring the local shrubbery, dreaming about how great life could be and totally ignoring Ryan.

Shit, Ryan. I've been too busy dreaming. I should be making more of an effort to talk to him, or hold his hand or something, especially as things are likely to start getting a little bit heated in a minute or two.

'So, what star sign are you?'

I have no idea where that question came from, but I just needed something to say to break the ice while we are walking.

'Libra.'

'You?'

'Gemini'

'So you really are a true twin.' He winks at me and I feel myself get a little hotter under my dress.

He then stops in front of me on the pavement as if to make an important declaration.

'By the way I've been wanting to say something to you all evening but I was wondering whether you were going to realise it first. I'll give you a couple of seconds longer to see if you can figure it out.'

I look him up and down; maybe this guy is more emotional than I thought. Maybe he wants to tell me that he likes me and thought that I would've recognised his signals. Any guy would have to spell it out to me; I am clueless about these things. Then I wonder if he is actually going to give me bad news. Maybe I've been catfished or something. God dammit I knew this guy was out of my league. I knew it was too good to be true.

'You haven't twigged yet, have you?'

I shake my head as if I am a naughty child and hope that what he is about to say doesn't ruin this evening.

'We've caught eyes before, at the rather classy establishment known as Juicy Parrot.'

'Oh my god, it's you. To be honest I think I just blocked out everything to do with that place. Just to clarify your friend is a complete dick. And I will never set foot in that place again.'

'Just to clarify, he isn't my friend; he is what I call an associate. And you're right, he is a dick. But the Juicy Parrot is great fun.'

'Well, we'll have to agree to disagree. Anyway, as you have now found out for yourself, I am not a lesbian. My sister is, which was why I was raging at that guy for being so thoughtless.'

'Oooh Ruby you are definitely hinting at a saucy threesome now, telling me that your sister is a lesbian.'

'And you are definitely cruising for a bruising,' I reply.

'Hey I am down for that weird S&M shit if you are.'

I let out a laugh. This guy is funny, albeit a bit persistent on the sex front. I grab hold of his hand and we walk as if we have known each other for years towards the entrance of the hotel.

The hotel is magnificent, easily Five Star with its red carpet and crystal chandeliers in the entrance. I almost feel like I am in some glamorous Hollywood movie from the 1950s. Ryan must've cottoned on to the fact that I was slightly in awe of the place.

'If you think this is fancy, wait until you see the bedroom,' he whispered in my ear.

This certainly beats Wally's hostel. I cannot wait to see the bedroom, although probably not for the same reasons as Ryan. I take a mental note of all the deep hues of burgundy and green in the reception and the polished wooden desks and marble floor and I think how I can turn the view of the hotel lobby into a drawing. I do actually have a small sketchbook in my bag but I don't want to blow my chances with him thinking I'm a weirdo by bringing a sketchbook out on a date.

I begin to tremble slightly. This is exciting, and that it was worth the risk to follow Ryan to this hotel. He could still be a murderer though. Look at those Agatha Christie and Miss Fisher novels. They were all set in swanky places like this.

Before I think of all the possible ways Ryan could murder me in this hotel, I find myself at the reception desk where Ryan is handed a key card. So he wasn't lying. He really does have a room in this palace. This is real. I think I am going to hyperventilate.

I feel Ryan's hand on my back, guiding me away from the reception and upstairs. I realise I've just gone back into daydream mode, and was therefore inadvertently gazing at the reception guy. Awkward.

As we get to the sixth floor, he places the key card in one of the dark mahogany doors and as he opens it I am greeted with a slice of pure interior design heaven. There is a large four poster double bed in the centre of the room, with what looks like pure Egyptian cotton sheets on top. I press my hands into the bed and they touch pure comfort. At either side of the bed are two art deco lamps, oozing with grace and sophistication. At the foot of the bed there is a beautiful bureau with a green leather seat. I make a note to myself that I must draw something whilst sitting at that bureau. It is just too good not to be used.

I peep into the bathroom. It is just as luxurious as the bedroom. I then head towards the window and pull back the curtains. The view is magnificent; Sydney at its best with all the city buildings glistening like diamonds in the dark with the harbour the jewel in the crown.

Suddenly I feel Ryan's hands snake across my waist and pull me in tight as he decorates my décolletage with light kisses. I melt like butter and kiss him fully on the mouth. I feel him calmly push the dress off my shoulders and move his hands across my breasts and in return I unbutton his shirt and before too long we are both without clothes and inhibitions. He pushes me gently on to the bed, and as I gaze into his eyes, I see the lust blazing in his eyes as I let my hands wander across his beautiful body.

I need to stop. As much as I am enjoying the strength of his arms, him holding me tight around the waist as he strokes my thighs, I just have to stop this before I get disappointed. Not disappointed sexually - my god, just the touch of his lips on my pale sun-deprived body sent tingling sensations to places I never thought possible. No. I mean disappointed in what this will be become. This amazing time of laughing, flirting and breathing in the vitality of life and then waking up the following morning to find the guy who seemed like your world last night has just disappeared.

No. I can't have this happen again. I am looking for real love not just a one night stand.

'This doesn't feel right Ryan,' I say, pushing him away gently. 'This is a first date. I think we should just leave today's adventure here before we spoil what fun we have already had.'

That sexual energy that had previously coursed through his body disappears in an instant, along with his smile. He looks disappointed. He just whispers a disheartened 'okay' and lets go of me as if I was some sort of rag doll before he rolls over to his side of the bed. I wonder if he was sulking or angry. Neither of those moods are what I want.

I roll in the opposite direction and my head starts swimming with thoughts. Why did you stop, Ruby? What happened to living in the moment? For Christ's sake, he's seen you naked, what difference would have sex make? You've made your decision so stick to it, don't be someone's play thing.

I still feel uneasy and even though I am sleeping in the most comfortable bed ever it does not provide any rest for my racing thoughts. I roll back towards Ryan and attempt to spoon him whilst whispering in his ear: 'If you are up for date number two then I might be able to offer you more'.

I immediately feel like some sort of cheap whore, offering

myself up on our next date. Yet despite the tension and competing thoughts I keep myself in the spooning position and hold my arm tight against Ryan's chest and prepare myself for a long night of over-thinking.

I must've finally gone to sleep as I awake with another pounding headache, a running theme during my short time in Sydney so far. My body is still cocooning Ryan. I gently roll away and begin working out the best way to leave this now awkward date to an end.

 I look back over at Ryan and see that he is still fast asleep. I don't want to leave while he is still sleeping as part of me still secretly hopes that this date can somehow be salvaged, and that a second date is possible. At the same time I don't want to look like some awkward hanger-on, waiting for him to call the shots if it was clear he just wanted my company for one evening only.

After weighing up my options I decide to wait until he wakes up and then I can make some feeble excuse about meeting my sister for breakfast.

I put on my clothes and head to the bathroom to splash cold water on my face in the hope it will make me feel better and clear my head. I make myself comfortable on the cool green leather seat and sit on the bureau I one day wish to own and bring out my sketchbook.

And then everything feels calm. I let my pencil glide across my sketchbook page and capture the pure magic of yesterday evening. I draw the grand hotel lobby with guests wearing ball gowns and tuxedos, bringing the hotel to life on the page in front of me. As I revel in how the page is coming together I hear Ryan's voice boom across the room and it makes me jump and almost draw a dark line across my drawing.

'What are you doing?' He leaps out of bed and charges over in his naked glory and before I can stuff my sketchbook out of sight and into my bag, he grabs it with both hands and looks through all the pages.

I am mortified. I sit there with baited breath awaiting his response, most probably a huge burst of laughter as to how bad the drawings are.

He looks at me and then back at the sketchbook and then towards me again before he responds.

'These are pretty good y'know. Have you ever had any published?'

I go a deep crimson and just shake my head. He is clearly being nice to spare my blushes.

'I don't think they are good enough, I doubt anyone would find them of interest.'

'Well I like them and I think you should put yourself out there more Ruby, you clearly have a talent so make sure people see it.'

Nobody has ever said I was talented before and I feel overwhelmed and at a lost as what to say and do next. Ryan breaks the silence.

'Right, I am not wasting my time here any longer; I'm dying for a bite to eat so I'll see you off at the hotel entrance so you can get on with your day as well.'

Wasting his time? Seriously I didn't force him here. This guy is such a Jekyll and Hyde. One minute he tells me I am gifted and the next that I am a time waster. Jesus. He clearly has issues. On the plus side it saved me making a feeble excuse to leave.

He quickly dresses with his back to me as I sit there waiting and hoping that something will happen to make things better between us. It doesn't. Ryan grabs his crumpled suit jacket from the floor and dusts it down before putting it on. He then strides straight up to me and looks me in the eye.

'This is yours. Do something useful with it?'

He presses the sketchbook firmly into my hands and I feel a slight electric shock from his touch and his green-eyed stare sends a shiver down my back. But before the spark even has a chance to develop he has already gone towards the door and opened it.

'After you,' he says coldly.

I want to scream. I've never received such mixed signals in such a short space of time. I am totally googling Schizophrenia when I leave as I swear he must be suffering from some sort of personality disorder.

As we leave the hotel he kisses me on the forehead and tells me that he will text me later and then disappears. I leave the hotel and head in the opposite direction wondering whether I need to visit a psychotherapist to explain what has just happened.

CHAPTER 12

She's back at the questions again. Just as I thought I would get a moment's peace from her interrogation on the walk from the bar to the hotel, she fills the air with her voice again.

Luckily this time the question was an easy one to answer as it was just about star signs, plus I had the bonus of giving her a saucy response while asking what sign she was. Chicks seem to really dig that horoscope stuff. No idea why. Just bullshit.

Despite her seemingly curious mind, I cannot believe she has got this far into the date and she has no idea that we met before. That's the thing with women; they end up being so self-absorbed that they don't see what's going on right in front of them. And people wonder why I don't want to get into serious relationships when all women are interested in is looking after themselves and getting a man to pander to all their needs while they live in their bubble.

I feel rather cruel teasing her, but I am enjoying watching her squirm a little and giving her something to think about. I give her a minute to try to remember where we had seen each other before, but she looks like she spontaneously combust if she thinks about it anymore.

I tell her we met at Juicy Parrot (or as I like to call it 'BPC' otherwise known as 'Backpacker Pussy Central'). I didn't tell her I call it that, don't think she'd appreciate it and I don't want to ruin my chances of getting laid tonight.

She takes in a sharp intake of breath as soon as I mention the words 'Juicy Parrot' and I can see as she looks me up and down that all the memories of that night come flooding back to her.

Her nose then slightly crinkles as if she has smelt a bad smell and then she begins to rant about Pete's douche bag cousin. I agree with that he is a douche bag, and that he also wins the title of 'lady repellent'. As soon as a woman gets a sniff of him they turn their noses up. Unless of course they're almost paralytic and extremely desperate. That does sometimes happen.

Then she drops the bombshell that her sister is a lesbian. I just imagine the two making out in front of me and then making out with me. Now that would be a good night.

I can feel another semi coming on already and we haven't even got to the hotel room yet.

I put the idea of a threesome out there jokingly, just to see if there might even be the slightest possibility of one, I can see from her face that idea is definitely KO'd. The semi is KO'd too.

I was secretly a little bit excited to see her reaction when we got to the hotel as it is a beautiful place and much better than the grotty little hostel she is probably staying in. As soon as we get to the entrance I see Ruby's mouth open a little in awe, and then close again into a smile of happiness as she takes in all the intricate wood carvings on the outside and on the entrance door.

I gently touch her back and guide her through the hotel's revolving door into the lobby. It looks like something out of the roaring twenties with polished marble floors, glistening chandeliers and brass sculptures. I look back at Ruby and she's like a wide-eyed child in a sweet shop as she takes everything in.

This is probably the best hotel in Sydney. Everything about it is incredible. When my mother first told me about it two years ago she described it as 'simply divine, darling', which is high praise from a woman as well travelled as she is. Thanks to all her book tours and TV appearances, she's stayed in the best hotels across the world. The hotel manager here is one of her adoring fans, falling in love with her when 'Make Love Last' was published. She stays here once a month, but sometimes if she has to miss a visit for work she lets me use her room. Suits me. I can live like a Prince for a while.

At times like these I could kiss my mother. She may have psycho-analysed my childhood to death, but she does have her more human moments. And she also gets some pretty awesome perks for what pretty much boils down to being an agony aunt to all the desperate and crazy women in the world.

I whisper in Ruby's ear that the bedroom looks even more amazing, just to confirm to her that that is our final destination. She melts further into a dreamy state and begins to almost glide along to the front desk. Her trance is broken by the concierge who asks her if she would like some assistance. She immediately hunches her shoulders, as if she is about to be attacked. I stifle a laugh. Most of the girls I bring here are smug and have a sense of entitlement. But this girl feels like a fish out of water. The thing is, of all of them, she's the one that probably fits here the best.

I step in and take charge and the concierge hands over the key to suite 612. I almost feel like Richard Gere in Pretty Woman. Shame Ruby isn't wearing some sexy PVC knee-high boots. But considering the first thing I want to do is get naked; the boots might've been more of a hindrance.

Ruby appears to be in a state of shock, so I put my hand on her back in order to move her along. The more time spent in the lobby means less time in the bedroom. Now I've got the key the excitement is really building and I am just desperate to get the clothes off our bodies. The lift to the sixth floor seems to take eternity but with every floor we go up, I feel something else in my trousers go up as well.

We make it to 612 and as I open the door to the suite I hear Ruby take a deep breath.

She walks around the room her eyes gleam with delight and there is a slight skip in her step. She seems mesmerised as she explores the room, inspecting the bathroom and then pushing the curtains at the window apart to admire the stunning view of the city at night. As she gazes out, I take the condom from my wallet and put it on the bedside table in readiness, and then walk up behind her and circle her waist with my arms.

I know she can feel the hardness in my trousers as I caress her elegant neck with kisses. As she succumbs to my touch, she moves her hand from the curtains so that they fall closed again, and turns around. She pushes her body fully against mine, deeply kissing my mouth. My hands slide her dress off her shoulders until her bra is exposed and then her dress falls to the floor.

I begin to undo the belt buckle on my trousers as she starts unbuttoning my shirt. Within moments our clothes are in a crumpled mess together on the floor and we are already tearing at each other's underwear. I push her down on to the bed so and let my hands explore the whole of her body. Such beautiful pale body with hips that have the right amount of curve and breasts that need the attention of my hands.

Her hands on my body are gentle yet firm, gripping just where they need to in order to increase the pleasure. The foreplay is intense and I wonder how long I can go on for before needing to reach for the condom and get deep inside her.

Then suddenly she stops. She lets me go, her hands and mouth removed from my body. I feel like I have been doused with cold water. I wonder if it is some kind of joke. Is she teasing me? Or have I done something wrong? Or maybe she thinks my dick looks like a potato. I take a quick look and it looks just fine to me, though certainly less erect than it was a few minutes ago.

Looks like Ruby has decided that's my lot. Her hands are now resting behind her back and she has made a small space between us. I don't push her to go further. I'm not a monster and would never force a girl to do anything she doesn't want. I let out a deep sigh and I turn over to the side and pretend to sleep.

This is the first girl to ever get this far and turn me down. Ah, Gemini. Switching from saucy twin to sensible twin. My mother always said be careful with Gemini's...Oh god why I am thinking about my mother at a time like this. Just go to sleep Ryan. But then she curls her arm around me, and though my initial impulse is to bat her away as I would normally do, I let her stay there in the spooning position, finding the feeling of her body against mine and her arm tight around my chest surprisingly comforting.

She whispers in my ear that maybe next time might be the time I get to fuck her. I think she's just trying to make things better, but I doubt she means it. I might take her up on her offer another time if nothing else is available. But for now I close my eyes and pray for sleep so that this rather unsatisfactory and confusing night can come to an end.

*   *   *

I must've dozed off as when I re-open my eyes I see that the clock says 8am. I look down my chest and see that Ruby's arm is still wrapped tightly round my chest. I stare at the arm and think about all the ways I could move it without disturbing her in order to escape but just before I put any plan into action I feel the arm snake away from my body.

Looks like Ruby might be beating me too it in trying to get out of here. I decide to close my eyes again and pretend I am still asleep, allowing her to make a swift exit and avoid any awkward 'about last night' chat. I hear her putting back on her clothes and the sound of the bathroom tap running. I then hear the scraping of furniture as if she is moving it out of her way to get to the exit. I brace myself for the sound of the door clicking to open and close but as much as I strain my ears I hear no noise.

I count to one hundred in my head and still I hear no sound of movement or doors closing. I begin to wonder if she was just super quiet when she left and I didn't hear her. Or maybe I have become deaf at the grand old age of twenty seven. Perhaps she has flown out of the window like Superman? I roll over onto my back to see if she has flown back to Krypton. But she is still here.

She is sitting at the bureau in the room. Her left hand seems to be moving frantically and as the hand is on the table I rule out the possibility that she is engaging in some early morning masturbation. Which is a shame. I then see that she is holding a pencil, and it then dawns on me that this girl might not be as sweet and innocent as she looks. She could be one of those fucking tabloid journalists out to dish some dirt on my mother. Only a few weeks ago she's was on billboards around Sydney promoting her new chat show as if she is the Australian equivalent of Oprah Winfrey.

I feel such an idiot. I should've checked her out in more detail. I bet she is loving the fact that Doctor Lara Turner's son doesn't believe in all this relationship guff she promotes and is only interested in one night stands.

I decide to stop her in her tracks and rat her out. I push the bed sheets back from me and leap from the bed, roaring towards her.

She looks like a rabbit caught in the headlights as I grab hold of the small leather bound book she has been writing in to see exactly what she's up to. But she hasn't written a single word. Instead there is a sketch of the hotel lobby downstairs and it is probably one of the best sketches I have ever seen. I've pissed myself off now. I let myself jump to conclusions.

As I flick through the pages, Ruby looks mortified, as though I am reading the pages of her teenage diary so I deliberately take my time to pour over the images, knowing that it is making her uncomfortable, but also because I am taking in their beauty. She says she's never had anything published. She is truly talented and I tell her that she should do something about that.

Talent should not go to waste. Which is why I make sure I show all the girls my talents. Ha. I sound so vain, but without the confidence I have gained over the years I wouldn't have had so much fun. As she turns her back on me to pick up her bag and to start to make an exit out of here, I take the opportunity to tear out the picture of the hotel lobby and quickly shove it in my pocket before giving her back her sketchbook.

I immediately feel guilty for stealing one of her sketches, so I try to make a swift exit so she doesn't have time to realise the drawing is gone whilst I'm still with her. I keep answers short and to the point. Besides I'm still a bit peeved that I didn't get laid so I am not going to be that nice to her this morning.

Eventually I get dressed and we head down to the lobby where I give her a peck on the cheek and tell her I will text her. I won't.

The girl always texts first, I text them back saying see you later, and that's the end of the story. Although last night was interesting. And confusing. And I would like to know if she really would offer me another chance for a slice of cherry pie.

I shrug it off, text Chad to see if he wants to grab a beer later tonight at the Oaks. I don't think I'll bother with finding a Miss Sunday.

CHAPTER 13

Why? Why, do I still feel the need to see this guy again? He clearly doesn't see me as girlfriend material. Yet I want to find out if there is more to Ryan than his Mr. Lothario act. I cannot text him. It would look desperate. I mean, I am desperate. But even I have standards.

Besides it's 4:50am, and no one should be texting at this time in the morning. In fact no one should even be up at this ungodly hour. But needs must, and I really can't afford to fuck up what might be this might be my only chance of getting a job and getting enough money to get out of that hostel. I swear I have been bitten by something lurking in those threadbare yellowing sheets as my arm looks and feels red raw.

I walk down the steps of Martin Place Station bleary eyed and itchy but as I get to the station forecourt and see the mini Babylon before me known as 'Fascinating Florals' I already feel a sense of happiness. It was an illusion that didn't last long. Tess barks at me as soon as she sees me.

'What time do you call this Ruby?' Her arms are crossed in front of her chest.

My stomach plummets to the floor; I swear I am on time. Maybe I misheard the time and it was actually 4am…oh god…I might as well go home now. No it was 5am. I wrote it down. I am definitely not late.

I decide this job means too much right now for me to just walk away as I really need the money. I take a deep breath and for once in my life, I stand up for myself.

'It's 4:57am, you did tell me 5am,' I quiver back to her.

'That's right, and I love someone who is punctual.' She lets out a hoarse laugh and then punches me on the arm. 'I had ya going for a bit there didn't I?'

'Just a bit.' I reply nursing my throbbing arm, which now makes a match for the other one.

'Okay let's get cracking, these flowers don't sell themselves,' she says to me more seriously, thrusting a bucket of tulips into my hands.

The work is more physically demanding than I thought, and there are so many different names for all the flowers, and there is so much more to learn than I ever imagined. But despite feeling super tired I absolutely love it. The sweet smell that rises from the stall is intoxicating and the shapes and textures of the flowers are divine. I feel like I am going to really enjoy working here.

At 8am, Tess lets me have a break for breakfast and I head for the cafe just outside the station to get some porridge. And, sucker that I am, I check to see if Ryan has sent me a message. One message received. My heart starts pounding in my chest. Please let it be him. Please be Ryan. It isn't. It is Laurence.

I had almost forgotten about him. He was such a lovely guy and how I wish he was still in Sydney rather than in the arse end of nowhere. We might have stood a chance.

The message read: 'Good luck on your first day. I hope all is going well. I thought you might appreciate a selfie with my new breakfast buddies, Kylie and Jason. X'

I let out a snort of laughter as the selfie is him with two kangaroos and one of them appears to be wearing Laurence's sunglasses.

I have a quick conversation with him to say thanks and to update him as to how things are going, but avoid mentioning Ryan. Just as when we were face to face the conversation just flows and I find it so easy to talk to him. Just as my mind starts to wander into 'getting married and having kids' territory, he shatters my dreams by mentioning someone called Sam. He is sharing a room with Sam. Sam is clearly a girl. Sam takes an age in the bathroom. I let out a sigh and lament that the good guys are snapped up so quickly and end the conversation, ready to head back to work.

It was nice of him to text though, and it is good to have a friend like Laurence. Even if I can't put the word 'boy' in front of the word 'friend.'

'You have a bit of a glow about you after your brekky break,' shouts Tess as I walk back down the steps into the station.

'You weren't chatting up the guy behind the brekky counter were ya? If you're not careful you'll end up spending all your wages in there trying to impress that boy.'

I look at her slightly shocked and embarrassed as the guy behind the counter at the cafe looked about seventeen and his skin was covered in so many pustules, it looked like it had more chance of erupting at any second than Mount Vesuvius.

Tess lets out another throaty laugh.

'Only joking. God sometimes you Pommies need to lighten up.'

I grin and try to think of a good comeback or a funny joke to throw back to Tess but my mind is blank so I decide to bury my head in the gladioli and pretend I am sorting them out in colour order.

Tess however, comes up really close and I try to think of something witty to say so that she will hopefully back off a little. Although so far the only joke I can think of is; 'Why did the chicken cross the road?' I don't think I will be winning any comedy awards with that one.

I can now feel her breath on my cheek and it's making me feel really uncomfortable.

'Now on a more serious note,' she whispers in my ear. 'I am promising that this time I am not joking…see that man standing in the kiosk opposite. I suggest you stay away from him as I just have a bad vibe about that one.'

I look over to where she is indicating and see a guy serving a commuter in the newspaper and sweets kiosk. He is of a slim build with slicked back blonde hair and big thick black rimmed glasses that make his otherwise baby-face seem older, although he is probably in his mid-thirties.

He seems harmless enough although Tess seems to think otherwise.

'The guy's name is Michael, that guy gives me the heebee jeebies. I don't know why, but there is something not right about him. I've seen the way he has looked at Carmen before and I don't like it. I suggest be polite when he comes over to us but keep contact with him to a minimum.'

Thankfully a customer comes along to break up the conversation. I'm sure that Michael isn't as bad as Tess is making out. He seems popular with the commuters, as there has been a non-stop queue outside his kiosk this morning.

My first customer of the day is a middle - aged business man with greying hair and a paunched stomach. He buys a bunch of red roses, not for his wife but for his mistress. Or at least, he said these were for his mistress. He might have been joking. Between train arrivals, the station is quiet and the stall is quiet. I take a moment to breathe and look around the station. There's not much to it other than the convenience store opposite us, the electronic train ticket machines and the ticket barriers before the platforms. Our stall is the only source of colour in an otherwise very dull, grey building.

Suddenly a large herd of people surge towards the ticket barriers and a barrage of beeping fills the air as they tap their tickets on the machine to enter the station. It's like the start of the zombie apocalypse. Each commuter looks tired and spaced out as they go through of the motions of tapping their travel card against the machine and walking mechanically to work.

Amongst the zombies I spot a man who, despite the tiredness round the eyes, looks rather handsome and is wearing a rather nice tailored navy suit. Something makes me think I have seen that style somewhere before.

Oh Christ, that's Ryan. And he is heading straight towards me. I really do not need him on my first day, especially as I feel I am doing so well even if I can't work out Tess's jokes. The more I am pleading in my head for him to turn around or just disappear into thin air the closer he is getting.

'Hello Ruby,' he grins as he stands in front of me almost toe to toe.

I literally want to die right now.

'Hey,' I respond, trying to act natural but failing by miles.

'I've come to buy some flowers,' he says confidently with a poker face.

Bastard. He didn't even ask how I was or whether I got home okay after we parted ways yesterday morning. Instead he wants to buy a bunch of fucking flowers for some other girl. I am absolutely fuming right now. I try to ask some subtle questions, I might have gotten the wrong end of the stick. They could be for his mother.

'So Ryan, who is the lucky lady?'

'You probably know her. Help me pick out a suitable bunch of flowers for her.'

I know her? Who else would know Ryan…oh good god, maybe he shacked up with Party Pam.

I am finding it really hard just to choose a bunch as my head is swimming. Thankfully Tess has come to my assistance and fills the air with her deep and calming voice;

'Maybe you should get ya girl a big bunch of roses, most girls like roses from a man.'

'Yes that sounds perfect.' He flashes Tess one of his winning smiles and I can immediately see she is smitten. He is such a player.

'I am sure Ruby will be able to wrap the bunch up all fancy for ya.'

Oh will I now Tess? Yes of course, I'll go and wrap up a bunch of roses for that toss bag who just went on a date with me just the other day, who has failed to text me and is clearly romancing some other girl. No problem at all. I really hope the girl who receives them gets stabbed with each and every single thorn when she unwraps them.

'So Ryan, who would you like me to write the card out to?'

He grins slyly and the name that comes out of his mouth surprises me.

'Ruby.'

Ruby? How the hell did he manage to find another girl in the city with the same name as me? This is unbelievable. It's not like my name is that common. I look up at him with my pen still poised as if this is some sort of wind up.

'Don't look so shocked Ruby. They're for you. Although you can only collect these later tonight. Meet me at Gino's Restaurant tonight at 7pm. I'll text you the details.'

Ryan grabs hold of the bunch of flowers and casually drops fifty dollars on to the counter, ten dollars over the asking price. He tells me to keep the change. He then walks back into the zombie march towards the station steps to the outside and into the city.

As soon as he disappears from sight I curse myself for standing like a rag doll and not coming up with a cool response. When I hear an 'ooooooooooohhhhh' sound from Tess and I feel my face burning up and prepare myself for more jokes at my expense. But I don't really care. I am too busy thinking about date number two.

CHAPTER 14

I have never known so much fuss about a bunch of flowers. The guys at work had an absolute field day wondering who they were for and whether they were actually a present to me from some boyfriend I had in Hawaii called Chuck. They clearly have too much time on their hands and not enough work to do. Most of the stick came from Paul. But while Paul's closest companion this evening will be his own hand, mine will be a beautiful and pert woman by the name of Ruby.

The look on her face was priceless when I ordered those flowers, even if I did pay $10 over the asking price. Flowers are so bloody expensive, but I didn't want to look like a cheap arse and wait for the change, it would've ruined my 'suave' image.

Thankfully she didn't see me trip up the stairs a few moments later due to the flowers blocking my vision as that would've killed the vibe completely.

I had no idea she worked there. I don't normally get off at Martin's Place, it's only because of yet another delay to the train service that I decided it would be easier to walk from here than struggle on to the next stop.

Is it fate that I saw Ruby…. nah, just coincidence.

I double check that the flowers are still in good condition as I walk towards the restaurant, knowing full well I am fifteen minutes late. That's one of the first rules of the dating game - never be on time. Showing you are too keen gives a girl the chance to wrap you round your little finger. The last thing I want to be is someone's bitch. I am always top dog.

I see Ruby opposite the restaurant. She looks stunning with her short light blue denim jacket and flowy white summer dress which is showing off a good portion of her slender legs. It's almost as if she is a Greek goddess with her golden curly locks tumbling down her back. She's definitely hot with a capital 'H'.

She spots me and walks towards me and despite my intention to give her a hug, I end up shoving the bunch of flowers right in her face. I swear to god these flowers are more trouble than they are worth. I better be getting a serious seeing to tonight to make this effort worthwhile. I blame nerves for my poor greeting effort, although I am never nervous so maybe it's the copious amounts of coffee I had to drink today at work that is putting me on edge.

As I pull the bunch of flowers out of her way in order to give her a proper greeting, she lets out a huge sneeze. The beginning of the date is almost like a Mr. Bean sketch and we're not even at the restaurant yet. I let out a loud laugh at the hilarity of it all and I hand her my handkerchief in case she sneezes again.

It must be the first time I have ever used the handkerchief for its proper purpose. It's probably the first time I have helped a girl out like that. Normally I leave it to them to sort their shit out.

She hands me the handkerchief back, although now that she has wiped her nose on it I am not sure I want it, but I stuff it back in my pocket without saying anything and guide her to the entrance of the restaurant.

I ask her if she likes Italian. I see her eyes light up but her mouth reacts differently as she responds.

'Italian is okay.'

I know she likes it but is trying to act be cool. Let's see how cool she acts when I tell the restaurant owner, Gino, her response.

Gino's restaurant is bloody amazing. It is hands down THE best Italian in Sydney. As soon as you enter the front door your senses go into overdrive with the smell of fresh pasta cooking, chopped herbs and juicy tomatoes followed by the sweet smell of a homemade tiramisu.

And then there is Gino himself, a real character. He strides towards us and as he gets closer he realises it's me and I see a big grin cracking over his moustachioed face.

I first came to Gino's to discuss accounts with a client over dinner two years ago and as a result ended picked Gino up as a client as well. When he provides such amazing food it's hard to say no to come and visit and check the numbers add up positively to keep this place going. Although the place is amazing it doesn't always get the footfall from passing trade, which is why you can generally get a table here without the need to book.

Before I drift too much back into work mode, Gino nudges me back into the present by giving me a big bear hug. I give him a strong hug back followed by the usual pleasantries whilst regaining my composure after being lifted several feet off the floor by Gino.

While we show off our manly love to the whole of the restaurant I see that Ruby is looking a little awkward and confused as to what she has witnessed, so I decide to press her embarrassment button by telling Gino who she is and that she thinks Italian is 'okay'.

As soon as the words come out of my mouth I see Ruby's cheeks turn crimson. I have a feeling tonight is going to be a lot of fun.

Gino starts waving his hands about as if he is washing an imaginary car and then finishes off his animated speech with a kiss of his fingers. This guy is hilarious. After every diner has turned around to look at Gino and hear how great Italy is, Gino then decides to show us our seats for the evening.

I pull out a chair for Ruby and before she can sit down, I begin with the questions. Question after question. In her polite British way she answers each and every one very politely. And surprisingly I actually liked listening to what she had to say about things, maybe because she didn't once feel the need to tell me what her 'shoe of the week' is or when her next hair appointment is.

After a while Ruby struggles to keep up but as if by magic Gino appeared to take our order, and Ruby hastily chooses from the menu. It probably didn't help that I gave her no time to read the menu properly. I know exactly what I want so sometimes forget other people need to see what's on offer. She chooses Spaghetti Bolognese. In my head I give her the thumbs up as I always choose Bolognese the first time I visit an Italian restaurant as you can always judge an Italian restaurant as to how well they make it.

I go for my usual Tagliatelle Dei Leccessi. I love how Italian I sound when I say it although Gino is probably crying inside as I butcher his beautiful language.

Gino then points us in the direction of the drinks menu and I leave it up to Ruby to decide for us. Gino then gives me the wink as we both recall what happened last time I let a girl order wine here. She ordered a bottle of Merlot, grabbed the bottle, glugged it down in one and stumbled straight out of the restaurant and into a taxi waiting outside.

Thankfully she has been the only crazy one I have picked up on GirlmeetsBoy. I like to think I have quite a good bogan detector, but this one slipped through the net. I gave Gino a rather handsome tip and a big apology and either the dollars or the fact that he had seen this behaviour from women before meant he ended up seeing the funny side of it all.

Ruby doesn't look like a girl who would do that. Well I hope not anyway.

A minute or so passes and Ruby still hasn't ordered. Jeez, either this girl is super picky or she is just super clueless with wines. I look at her chewing her bottom lip and scanning the menu up and down. It looks like she falls in to the clueless category and a part of me feels bad for putting her in that position.

I recommend a good Aussie wine to her to help her out of her misery, plus I see that Gino's is getting fed up waiting as well so hopefully this will hurry her along. Thankfully she goes with my suggestion. If I had to wait any longer for her to choose I think I'd just go to the bar myself and get a bottle to glug down to help me through this agonizing wait.

As Gino goes and gets us the Shiraz, I decide to move the date along a bit to get closer to my goal of getting her into bed with me. I lean over the table and whisper in her ear.

'You know, once you have had a taste of an excellent Australian wine, the best thing to follow it up with is the taste of an excellent Australian man, especially if he is called Ryan.'

My pulse is racing with excitement and it looks like hers is too as her pupils get wider and she appears more flushed. I wait to see if she is going to give me a sexy comeback, but Gino has already appeared with the glasses so she just ignores my comments and asks me to teach her about the differences in wine and what ones to choose.

I tell her everything I know about wines, and I impress myself about how much I actually know although I am starting to wonder if I come across like an old fart talking about the differences between Chablis and a Chardonnay. Yet Ruby appears to be enraptured as she sits closer into the table to listen to me and bats her big blue eyes in my direction showing she is taking in every single word. This girl is so different to the others. I so want to kiss her right now but Gino has placed a steaming hot plate of pasta in front of me.

My manners go straight out of the window as I scoff huge mouthfuls of the food into my mouth; it's too good to be sitting there for even a second.

After the third big mouthful of pasta, I look over to Ruby and wonder what an earth she is doing as she is cutting up her Spaghetti Bolognese into tiny pieces as if she is feeding it to a china doll. She then slowly lifts the fork with the tiny bit of pasta to her mouth as if she is stuck in slow motion.

I know that the English are known for the politeness and etiquette at the dinner table but seriously if she is going to eat the whole meal like that we will be here until next Tuesday. I cannot sit here and watch this weird way of eating so I decide to tell her to stop with this odd shit.

'Why are you eating so weirdly Rubes, just get stuck in, no need to worry about manners with me…. here I'll show you how you should eat it.'

I stick my fork right in the middle of her spaghetti Bolognese and twirl a large portion of the pasta mince and tomato sauce on my fork before slurping it in my mouth. I then notice that in my attempt to be bold in front of Ruby I have managed to get some of the tomato sauce on my shirt…that will teach me for being such an arrogant arse.

Luckily, I don't think Ruby noticed and if she does mention it I will just tell her it's not sauce but one of those fancy shirts which has weird orange and red patterns on it. Although if she believes that she is naiver than I thought.

Her eyes are gleaming at me as I finish my forkful and without hesitation she gives me a big grin and sticks her fork into her plate and takes a big mouthful.

The delight on her face encourages me to take another forkful of her food so I can see whether this can lead to something and in fact it does lead somewhere…right to Ruby's kissable lips. Like a scene from a movie we end up sharing the same string of spaghetti and as we are clearly people who do not like to give up we continue to eat until I plant a pasta filled kiss on her. It wasn't quite how you imagine it would feel like in the movies but it did give me a chance to see how up she was for 'sexy time' later.

Her response gets my pulse racing.

'Well seeing as you like playing with your food, I look forward to trying each other's desserts at yours later.'

I almost feel myself blush and something rise in my trousers but I keep my cool knowing I will need to save myself for later.

Before Ruby changes her mind and goes cold turkey on me I quickly summon Gino for the bill. As before, Ruby tries to offer to pay at least half but I refuse, she's too good to have to pay for anything in my company. It makes a change to spend my money on someone who is appreciative. Every other girl I've dated expects me to pay for everything without even pretending to offer.

Before I take her back to mine on the train, I decide to warm us both up by taking her for a walk by the botanic gardens. Its only five minutes from Gino's and it will help me calm my nerves a little. Something about this girl is giving me butterflies. Or maybe it is the mix of pastas turning in my belly. I can't work out why this girl is getting such a hold on me tonight, but I am hoping the gardens will have her feeling more relaxed too and ready to taste her dessert later.

As we get to the gates, it dawns on me that it won't be open as it's nearly dark. Luckily there is a bench just outside so I sit down on it and hope that Ruby does the same.

Like an obedient dog she sits but we both sit in silence, unable to break the tension between us. For once on a date I am really not sure how to make the next move. Normally I would just go straight in with a kiss making it clear my intentions.

I feel my dinner gurgling in my stomach and it gives me an idea which might just make it easier for me to start a full-on PDA session with her.

I turn to Ruby and tell her she has spaghetti sauce on her face. She doesn't have anything on her face at all, and even if she did she would still look pretty. She looks mortified, but as the helpful gentleman I am, I pretend to come to her rescue and wipe the imaginary sauce away.

I get closer and closer and eventually our lips touch and then after a while of massaging her soft lips with mine I then go for the tongue and just as I do, I feel a weird vibrating sensation on the top right hand side of my body. Ruby doesn't seem to notice and she is forcefully pushing her lips on me in order to continue with the kisses.

The vibration doesn't seem to stop. This is really distracting. I really can't deal with this anymore, maybe she is more into some kinky shit than I realised and has brought her vibrator along for tonight. Even so, now is not the time or place.

As I push her away to work out what the hell is vibrating in her pocket, she tells me it's her phone. I almost let out a laugh thinking how crazy I was to think it might have been a vibrator. Whoever it is, they are desperate to get hold of her so I tell her to answer it to put us all out of our misery. The vibrations stop before she answers and for a while she just stares at her screen.

'It's my sister.'

Maybe she is down for a threesome after all. It really would be my lucky night, although it is more likely her sister is probably menstruating or something. I presume that's what sisters talk about. As an only child, I never really understood the close sibling bonds people have. Surely people want to live their own life rather than constantly hanging around or dealing with their brother or sister problems?

'I think she might be in a bit of state as she needs me to meet her urgently,' she says, clearly concerned.

I fill the air with my frustration. She looks a bit startled, but I know my chance to sleep with her has gone and I don't care anymore even if I do come across as having a toddler tantrum.

Fuck sisters. Fuck Ruby. Oh wait I can't do the last one as she has some other bull shit excuse as to why she can't sleep with me. I knew it. I should've just left it at the one date like I normally do.

As I deal with my frustration Ruby manages to hail a cab to take her back to her sister. I say goodbye and begin sorting out a backup plan for this evening. It's time to ring Tanya.

Within three rings she answers and the booty call is sorted. There is a warm feeling again in my trousers and I am ready for action. But my head is full of confused thoughts about Ruby and our time together this evening.

CHAPTER 15

Martha better be fucking dying. I have yet again given up the chance to take things further with Ryan.

The night was going so well. Ryan was so kind over my embarrassing lack of knowledge about wine and was willing to share his knowledge so passionately on the subject. The restaurant owner, Gino was such a character too, he was like something out of the Godfather. Although I did wonder whether I would be mincemeat after Ryan told him I thought Italian was okay. I bloody love Italian, that will teach me for trying to play it cool with Ryan.

And even when I was eating my spaghetti Bolognese like a demented woman in order to avoid getting tomato sauce down my white dress, he told me not worry about it and enjoy the delicious food. I can still feel his warm and gentle kisses on my neck.

Everything was going so well; until Martha messaged.

He was in such a foul mood when I left. I doubt I will see him again, but my family have to come first.

Last time Martha sent me a text message like this, I arrived to find her howling like a toddler next to a big black splat on the road.

Smudge, our cat had been run over. I have never heard a grown woman shriek so hysterically. I suspect some of the local residents thought I was her carer and had been sent to calm her down and take her back to the home.

I never really liked Smudge. It has this evil glint in its eye as if it was going to expose all my deepest darkest secrets at any moment but to Martha it was her little side kick. Martha would rather have lost her arm that lost Smudge.

I had to spend the next fortnight comforting her and spending half my wages on Ben and Jerrys to make her feel better.

I do not want a repeat of that.

As the taxi drops me off at Sunshine Apartments, the location Martha told me to meet her, I see Martha and Chloe waving at me frantically and jumping up and down as if they are little school girls who have been fed too much sugar. So much for expecting to see Martha crying in a crumpled heap on the floor.

After receiving a big hug from Martha and Chloe the verbal diarrhoea from Martha begins. I catch snippets of the words that we are sharing a room…finding your own room in Sydney is like gold dust… good we get to share with each other rather than strangers…the live-in landlord is a bit of a creep but the three of us against him will put him in his place…

I try my best to take everything in but I am too busy thinking what if, what if I just ignored her message? What if I had asked Ryan to come with me?

A second chance like that doesn't come around often. I thought I had blown it on the first date by not letting go of my inhibitions and going all the way with him and tonight could've have been a chance to prove I really am carefree and fun and ready to explore the physical side of things with him.

'Ruby why aren't you happy? Chloe went to a lot of effort to get those beds for us. There is no need to be ungrateful,' Martha whines in my ear, handing me my key to the flat.

I try to prove to Martha that I really am happy by plastering on my best fake smile despite crying a little on the inside knowing that the chance for love is still too far away for me to grab.

Martha isn't buying the fake smile, she knows me too well dammit.

'Look sourpuss I have a surprise for you in our room, which will hopefully cheer you up'

Martha grabs my hand and the three of us bound up the stairs to the fourth floor and towards a door numbered 432.

A rather short angry looking Asian man greets us at the door in what appears to be an off-white string vest and a pair of board shorts.

'This your sister,' he says to Martha as he jabs his pointy finger into my shoulder. Martha nods her head.

'She pretty…really pretty.'

'Good to see you Mr Chen, how's your wife doing?' says Martha as she steps in between me and him so he can back out of my personal space.

'Oh, she good…I better go and let you girls get unpacked. I'll be in my room next door to yours so if you want me to view any of your party outfits then just let me know'

'I told you he was a creep, didn't I?' whispers Martha in my ear.

I nod my head and wonder what the hell possessed Martha to move us both here with creepy Mr Chen and wonder whether this is meant to be my surprise, being greeted by a perverted middle aged Asian man.

Martha again guesses my thoughts.

'Don't worry sis, that's not your surprise, I am not that cruel.'

She takes my hand and leads me into the flat and towards a door which I presume is our bedroom.

As I enter the bedroom, I see three basic single beds around the edge and Andre sitting crossed legged in the middle of the floor next to my rucksack eating a big slice of chocolate cake.

'Sorry Ruby, I was waiting so long for you to arrive I got hungry, so I hope you don't mind…maybe just view it as me being the tester to ensure you all don't get food poisoning.'

I laugh out loud. This is just typical Andre, such a funny sight sitting on the floor with chocolate round his mouth like a baby. I tell him not to worry and I sit down on the floor to join him in eating cake, even though I've had a big meal already. I can't say no to chocolate cake. Martha looks slightly mad that Andre had started on the cake already, but she just shrugs her shoulders and joins us. Chloe stares at us for a while and mutters under her breath but after some persuasion from Martha she eventually gives in and we all sit together talking and laughing.

Our evening of cake and conversation makes me feel warm and happy inside, although I do feel slightly guilty about being so ungrateful about the whole situation of finding a place to stay.

Just before we get ready to go to bed, and as Andre prepares to leave, I give each one of them a long and tight hug.

I feel lucky that I have such beautiful friends and family and it makes me realise that sometimes chasing after the love of a man shouldn't always be a top priority. The love of family and friends is always there and shouldn't be ignored, especially if that love comes with chocolate cake.

CHAPTER 16

It's nine o clock and I am holding up the side of the Opera Bar with my whisky in hand listening to another girl moan about how her ex-boyfriend didn't value her and didn't listen to what she had to say…blah…blah…blah. I am starting to get tired of listening to this crap and wish I had gone for the eager brunette on GirlmeetsBoy rather than this boring bleached blonde.

I even have my mother's hotel room again at the Sydney Skyscraper tonight but I am starting to question whether there is someone else on my phone list I can ring and share the hotel bed with as I doubt I will get much sleep if she continues to yak as loudly as she does. She looks like a snorer too. She is averagely pretty, even with all that hideous slap on her face but her nostrils are the size of the Grand Canyon. She probably makes enough noise to register on the Richter scale.

I think about Ruby sometimes and how she was so different, almost refreshing to these other ditzy and glamour obsessed girls. Believe it or not I am starting to get a bit sick of all this chasing around just for a one night stand which often end up mediocre at best anyway.

Suddenly I spot a wave of blonde hair pass me at the bar, her arm linked around some guy who clearly walked straight out of the Institute…the Mental Institute.

No it can't be…

CHAPTER 17

It's been six months since I have last seen or heard from Ryan and in those six months I have kept my social life busy with lots of dates with a lot of *weird* men. I am starting to think I have the settings on GirlmeetsBoy set to the frog category.

Although, I have managed to score quite a few nice dinners out for free even if the dates were terrible. A silver lining, I suppose.

I chastise myself for that thought as this isn't the Ruby of England, back home I would always pay for half and I would never go on dates with men I know were definitely bordering on the psychotic.

The last date I went on was with a guy called Spencer and he seemed to have some real potential as boyfriend material. He was well dressed, had a good job as a lawyer and had an interest in arts and culture. All seemed to be going well until after dinner when he decided to get out his box of floss from his jacket and began thoroughly flossing his teeth at the table and airing his tonsils to the world.

Then just as I thought the embarrassment of the flossing was over he then produced a small bottle of mouthwash from the same pocket on his jacket and then swilled it around his mouth before spitting it out into my water glass.

He then breathed all over my face just so I could check his breath was minty fresh. Seriously, there is a time and a place for oral hygiene and sitting at a restaurant table on a date isn't one of them. I did question him about it at the time but he just gave me this look as if I was the one who came from Psychoville. Thankfully I had just enough acting skills to convince him I had 'period pain' and needed to go back to my flat to lie down in order to make a swift exit. I pray that no one knew me in that restaurant.

The guy before Spencer was even more peculiar as he decided to speak in a mock-pirate accent throughout the whole of our date. He kept asking me whether I wanted to touch the 'Pretty Polly' in his trousers. I sometimes wonder where men get these ideas that acting like a very poor version of Johnny Depp's Captain Sparrow is the way to a woman's heart.

Before the perverted pirate I also went on a few dates with a guy called Garth and to be fair he was fairly normal in comparison to the others. Although he just would not shut up about his ex-girlfriend. The whole time it was 'Me and my ex-girlfriend did this...', 'I love it when my ex-girlfriend did this...' he just got seriously boring after a while banging on and on about her all the time so I decided to call time on our dates. I don't think he was too bothered as he's still probably pining for his ex-girlfriend.

All this online dating is so stressful. That's why today I have decided to make a very big decision. If this date doesn't go well then I am having a break from the dating game. In fact, I might start looking online for convents in Australia… okay maybe I won't become a nun but I won't rule it out after some of the men I met.

Instead I will focus on my true love; illustration. I've really enjoyed drawing all the beautiful flowers I work with, and I would love to sell the illustrations on Tess's stall if she lets me and I work up the confidence to show my work to someone else other than myself and Ryan that one embarrassing time. He said they were good and seemed to mean it. Or did he?

I let out a deep sigh as I sit on the steps of the Sydney Opera House waiting for my next date and my last hope at love. In midst of contemplating to myself, the state of my love life and the date I have tonight I get interrupted by a guy who looks like something out of a 1970s cop movie. He has brown hair which is heavily slicked back from his forehead and is wearing aviator sunglasses despite being dusk, a black shirt, leather jacket and neatly pressed black trousers. And most disconcerting of all, he has a big ugly moustache which looks like one of those fake ones you buy for the fancy dress store. Unfortunately his doesn't look like one you can just rip off.

Despite my initial shock at his appearance, he decides to continue speaking at me. His voice is of such a high pitch I wonder whether he has given the local birds a fright as well as me.

'Hi, my name is Pete; I believe you must be the beautiful Ruby?'

How the Dickens does this weirdo know my name?

Oh god have mercy, this guy is actually my date. He definitely doesn't look anything like the pictures he posted online. He certainly isn't scoring high with his looks and voice but I will give him top marks for his Photoshopping skills as he certainly convinced me he was handsome enough for a date, even with the moustache or maybe I was drinking too much of Chloe's sangria at the time to realise how much of an odd job this guy was.

Seriously Ruby, a guy with a moustache what were you thinking? That you were Princess Peach and he was going to be your Mario?

I have been spending way too much time on GirlmeetsBoy.

I confirm to my date that yes, I am indeed Ruby despite wanting to vehemently deny that it is me. I try to think positively as despite the outside maybe on the inside he has a beautiful personality. As my mother always told me, never judge a book by its cover. Although I also think she told me not to hang around with nut jobs.

He looks at me with his creepy green eyes and then proceeds to carry on talking to me in his unnaturally high pitched voice.

'Come, take my arm child. I shall escort you to the nearest drinking establishment where we will be merry and drink dainty drinks like little boys and girls at a tea party.'

Who talks like that? Also, I am not a child, what a creepy thing to say…. oh god maybe I am actually going on a date with a paedophile. Paedophile Pete. Jesus Christ Ruby, are you high? I need to get rid of this guy quickly, feign death if I really have to and just bloody get away from this fruit loop.

That slug across his face is enough to scare small children.

As I try to listen to my inner thoughts and plan my escape, somehow we get to the Opera Bar behind the Sydney Opera House for a drink, and then just as my evening can't get any worse, a ghost from the past turns up.

Looks like he is on a date as well, she looks his type too, blonde bimbo ready to bend over backwards for him. I pretend to not see him and hope he hasn't spotted me.

Bollocks. He is walking straight in my direction. No No No… please Ryan do not come over and gloat about how well your date is going and how I've ended up with Charles Bronson's weakly brother. Despite my best evil eye, Ryan is still walking straight to me with Paris Hilton's best friend on his arm. This guy is definitely being a dick with a capital D.

'Heeeyyyy Ruby, fancy seeing you here! Who's your friend?'

God he is one smug bastard. I see that Peter offers his hand as a way to introduce himself and Ryan just completely blanks him. Okay Pete looks and is strange but Ryan should at least be polite and shake his hand. I decide to have a dig at Ryan due to his rudeness.

'Oh hey Ryan, how's the Pet Detective business going?'

'Errr what are you on about Ruby, I work as an accountant you know that.'

'It was meant to be a joke Ryan as you look just like Ace Ventura in that tropical print shirt.'

Pete lets out a laugh and Ryan's face turns to thunder.

He looks peeved and rightly so. That's what he gets for gatecrashing my date and showing off like he always does.

'I'm Sasha by the way' pipes up the peroxide blonde.

Oh look the bimbo talks. No one asked for her input and I wish the two of them would just fuck off so I can make my escape from Pete and sit in my pyjamas with the girls at the flat and eat a big tub of ice cream and laugh at the ludicrous dates I find myself on.

Pete then grabs Sasha's hand and places a sloppy kiss on it.

'Please to meet you Sasha. Has anyone told you that you have beautiful brown eyes? They are just like Bambi's.'

WOW. This guy seriously is mentally ill. He is meant to be on a date with me but is giving another girl compliments and chatting her up. Ryan is clearly not happy about Pete's tactics either as he abruptly interrupts their conversation.

'Let's get some drinks, Ruby do you think you can give me a hand?'

I see that this could work to my advantage as it offers an escape route from Pete and as much as I'm hating on Ryan right now there is still something about him that pulls me to him and it would be nice to have a brief catch up and see what he is up to other than taking out questionable girls for drinks. Although I already have a feeling that I am going to be cursing myself later for agreeing to get drinks with him.

When we get to the bar Ryan looks back over his shoulder to where they are standing.

'Excellent they're not looking'. I'm guessing you are as desperate as me to get away from those two so let's take a quick left and get lost in the crowd. Thankfully its busy tonight as there is an open-air art exhibition just outside the Opera House. We can wait there for a bit until they give up looking for us and then we can head elsewhere.'

I nod in agreement, secretly pleased that he found his date a bore and also excited that I am about to do my first ever runner in the middle of a date.

He grabs my arm and I half walk, half run to get away from the Opera Bar as quickly as possible.

I think we are about to get caught red-handed.

'Hey! Guys where are you going…' shouts Pete.

Ryan pulls hard on my arm as he directs me to the left towards the Opera House where we go into a full pelt run until we get into the middle of the art exhibition. We are surrounded by a large crowd who are trying to get a glimpse of the artwork that is decorating the concrete plinths and floor of the harbour. I spot some souvenir photo booths at the far end of the exhibition and point Ryan in that direction also. He moves his hand from my arm and clasps it into my hand and we head straight to the booths.

Ryan barges into one of the booths shoving a teenage couple already in there and mid-pose for their souvenir shot out of the way and then pulls me in to the cramped booth where I become a jumble of hands and feet with the couple of being forced to move out of the way.

The couple are not happy with Ryan shoving them out like that and they are beginning to cause a stink which is attracting attention from the crowd. I try to apologise and claim its some sort of emergency, which they really aren't buying. I see Ryan reach for his wallet and pulls out some dollars, in fact it looks like about fifty dollars' worth.

'If I give this to ya mate will you bloody piss off?'

He shoves it in the pock-ridden boy's hand which finally makes the guy shut up. He tries to act like he's still annoyed by spitting on the ground but then he shoves the dollars in his jean pockets, takes his girlfriend's hand and as they walk away, he mutters;

'You can tell the guy's a douchebag if he pays people fifty dollars to do as he says....'

Ryan vehemently responds with a 'Fuck you', whilst I close the thin blue cotton curtain across the booth entrance and try to find a comfortable way to share the white plastic seat in the middle of the booth. I place a finger on his lips to quieten him as I can hear our names being shouted around the art exhibition and I try to calm myself down and breathe slowly in and out. The shouting of our names is getting louder. I decide to peep round the curtain which is separating Ryan and me from the outside world to see whether I can spot where they are and plan our next move.

As I look out I see that they are almost within touching distance of us but thankfully they have their backs to the booth. I briskly but quietly let go of the curtain and I put the whole of my hand across my mouth and my other hand on Ryan's mouth in the hope that it will stop all sound. I then close my eyes in the hope that when I re-open them they will all just disappear and that this is all just a figment of my imagination.

I listen intently to the sound of their voices.

'It looks like they have gone Sasha, Ruby did look a bit ill so maybe she had the shits and Ryan has gone to assist.'

'Really? I have a feeling they may have just ditched us.'

'Well either way they are going to be a while so why don't we cut our losses and go on a date together.'

'Sure, that would be cool. In fact my Dad owns a bar just a couple of streets away so we can go there and get our drinks for free.'

'Let's go my beautiful bambi.'

I wait a few more moments until I can no longer hear the clip-clopping of Sasha's shoes and release my hand from my mouth and the other hand from Ryan's mouth.

'That fucking bitch. She was trying to run me dry by ordering the most expensive drinks and her Dad actually runs a fucking bar.'

Ryan leans back on the booth seat and after a short pause lets out the most raucous of laughs.

'He thought you might have had the shits. Unbelievable. Well Ruby we sure do pick 'em.'

He raises his hand so I can give him a high five, which I do to show that our mission has been completed and then I re-cap the ludicrousness of our situation.

'Even worse is that he thinks you were assisting me! How? What were you going to do? Stand there and hold the toilet roll whilst the inside of my intestines shot through my backside?'

Ryan is now in stitches of laughter and is clutching his sides, which makes me go into hysterics also and causes us both to slide off the plastic chair and on to the photo booth floor. I haven't laughed like this in a long while. After a minute or so, we eventually regain composure and scramble back on to the plastic seat.

'Come on Ruby, let's go back to the Opera Bar and we can both have a cocktail and a guaranteed interesting conversation.'

Now would've been the time to tell Ryan to go do one after trying to be all friendly after he hasn't been in contact for six months but after the mini adventure we had together I have inevitably fallen for his charms again. However, I am feeling bolder than I normally do on dates so I decide to ask him for a picture as a memento of our interesting escape this evening.

'Why do you want one of those?' Ryan says defensively.

'Is it so you can finally have a picture to put in your shrine to me?'

'No I was going to use the picture of you as a dartboard' I respond sarcastically.

He begins to laugh again.

'Well in that case I better make sure I give you my best smile to ensure it's the best looking dartboard you ever have.'

We both squeeze closer together on the seat and whilst doing so I feel Ryan snake his arm around my waist and it sends shivers up my spine.

After what feels like an eternity we finally get to relax our smile muscles as the photo begins to print. Surprisingly, it looks like a nice picture. I'm sure Ryan always looks great in photos but I always end up looking like a cross between a scarecrow and Oscar the grouch. I quickly grab the photo from the dispenser and place it carefully in my purse before Ryan changes his mind and wants to get rid of it.

Ryan remains silent throughout which makes me question whether the photo was actually a really bad one and I'm just in denial. He removes his hand from my waist and places it in my hand and we clamber out of the booth and make our way slowly back to the Opera Bar.

*   *   *

Once arriving back at the Opera Bar, deep conversation and too many cocktails followed, so much so that Ryan gets a tap on his shoulder to say we are the only two left at the bar. I hadn't even realised that it was just us. Although it is late I don't want this evening between us to end just yet. I'm still plucking up the courage to ask if he fancies picking up from where we last left off on our previous date.

I suggest a walk around the Harbour before we part ways and before I even finish my sentence he agrees. I'm taken aback by his quick response but it gives me more confidence to ask him whether we want to continue things at his place. I'd suggest my flat but considering I share with two other girls I don't really want an audience and they probably won't want the noise or the images of naked bodies writhing about imprinted on their brains.

Clutching each other's hands tightly we walk from the Opera Bar round to the side where the black and white frontage of the Museum of Contemporary Art looks towards the water. Without saying a word and as if in sync we both sit on the bench in front of the museum and enjoy the darkness of the water stretched out in front of us.

For some reason I have an urge to start whistling Otis Redding's 'Sittin' On the Dock of the Bay. As I purse my lips and let the tune whistle in the air, Ryan automatically joins in.

I stop in surprise and feel my forearms begin to cover with goose bumps. This is a special moment. A connection of two people.

Ryan stops too and lets out a big grin.

'Why did you stop? This is a decent song… Is it because you don't know the rest of the tune?' he says mockingly.

I give him a look of 'please I know every part of that tune' and then simultaneously we both begin to whistle again picking up exactly where we left off.

As our whistling comes to a natural end, we both stare into each other's eyes and I see his pupils get bigger. We then break our intense gaze with a long and passionate kiss.

After the satisfying kiss, it seemed like the opportune moment to ask Ryan whether he want to take this further than just a romantic stroll and whistle.

'So, maybe I can go back to yours for coffee?'

As soon as I say the words 'back to yours for a coffee' I feel like a complete moron. It sounds like such a cliché thing to say, although saying 'do you want to have sex tonight?' sounds even worse and it makes me feel a little grubby so 'coffee' sounded like the best option even though it sounded like something out of an American TV show.

I await Ryan's reaction and at first he looks confused, looks like my coffee invitation wasn't clear enough. Then, as the penny dropped there was a look of a lost boy. Maybe I totally misjudged the situation. Yet on our previous dates he seemed to have sex on the brain, so what makes tonight so different?

He then shakes his head telling me that he has an important day ahead of him at work and needs to be on top form.

It seems to me like an excuse and I feel my gut tighten at the disappointment and the rush of adrenalin quickly fade away. I am unsure how to respond and an awkward silence ensues.

Ryan breaks the silence.

'Well it's probably time to grab some taxis and make our ways back separately.'

The word *separately* is deliberately emphasised by him to really make sure I understand that this night will not be going any further. Due to 'coffee gate' he is now unable to look me in the face. I feel like such a fool.

He walks me to a taxi and like a true gentleman pays the taxi driver. He then pops his head through the window as I put on my seatbelt and says to floor, in order to continue avoiding my eyes;

'Thanks for a good night Ruby, we will have to meet up again some other time… as friends'.

The word 'friends' sends a stabbing pain in my heart. As the driver begins to drive away, I look back at Ryan and he looks back at me. He then immediately turns his head away with not even a wave goodbye. As the taxi continues to drive to Sunshine Apartments, I feel my cheek become wet with the tears that are silently trickling down my face.

CHAPTER 18

I can't do it.

I just can't do it.

For the first time in my dating life, I can't go for coffee or sex, a three-course meal or whatever Ruby was insinuating because if I do I won't be able to control my feelings any longer and I am not talking about my sexual feelings. I promised myself I would never get attached to a girl and I would never fall in love. I'm getting too close to Ruby and this time it really does need to come to an end.

I gave Ruby some bullshit excuse of needing to be fresh and energised for work in order to leave and get out of the situation. I felt like such a douchebag but my mind has taken control of my heart.

As we stood by the harbour entrance I began waving my hands about to get a taxi for Ruby like an idiot, just panicking and out of control with my feelings. Once a taxi pulled up, I decided to make up for my rudeness and pay for her to get back okay but then I delivered the words no beautiful girl wants to hear from a guy she's dating; 'just friends'. My gut twisted as I said those words and Ruby's blue eyes were a midnight pool of sadness.

I tried not to look at her as the cab began to move away but I couldn't help it. When I looked back, I received another twist in my gut and had to tear my eyes away from her, away from her forever.

For once I am glad to be heading back to the hotel without anybody but myself. Not only does it mean that I can star fish on the bed, it also means I can sort out my thoughts and get back to the suave playboy version of Ryan rather than this stupid love-struck version of Ryan. It also gives my shredded arse a chance to recover from sitting on that white plastic seat in the photo booth. I wish she didn't have that picture of me, I never have a picture with any of the girls I have dated but somehow Ruby convinced me to have a picture with her.

I knew she was trouble as soon as she walked in. Oh for god's sake I am now even beginning to quote Taylor Swift songs because I've let my feelings for this girl take over me.

I curse myself for being such a pathetic loser as I continue to walk towards the hotel where I intend to order myself a large whiskey and to think about how many sexual positions I could do in a night with Taylor Swift, in order to get the thought of Ruby out of my head for good.

CHAPTER 19

It's been six weeks since I've heard from Ryan. I keep playing back our date again and again. I still can't work out what happened between us for him to turn me down. I think about all the possible ways I could've said things differently but it still doesn't change reality. I take a deep sigh and try to block out all my thoughts of him as clearly there is going to be no future between us.

Suddenly I get a slight jolt in my finger from a thorn on the rose I had been subconsciously twirling around my finger. That will teach me for staring into space and thinking about things I shouldn't rather than focussing on what I should be doing. I then realise that behind the large display of peonies I see a pair of well-polished black brogues and feel mightily embarrassed that I hadn't realised he was there and that I have been caught daydreaming at work. I am so glad Tess took the day off today otherwise I probably would've been fired on the spot there and then, even though sales these past few months have been rather good.

I go over to the smartly dressed feet to see if I can offer my assistance and my sincere apologies for ignoring him. I then realise that the customer is Michael, the guy who runs the newspaper and sweet kiosk. Normally Tess talks to him when he comes over, as he often gives us any left - over sweets he may have for the day. Other than smiling at Michael when he comes over, I do not talk to him as Tess tends to keep me busy when he is around as for some reason she thinks he might bundle me in a body bag at any moment.

I think Tess is majorly over-reacting, he hasn't really done anything particularly weird, other than only wearing polo necks even in the height of summer. Hopefully a bit of light conversation between us will be enough and he will return to his kiosk and will not mention to anyone that I was daydreaming.

'Hiya Michael.' I say cheerfully. 'I hope you haven't got any more of those Cherry Ripes to hand over as I am going to end up the size of a house at this rate.'

'Not this time I'm afraid', he replies back in his melancholic voice, '...although there is something I want to ask you. I hope you won't be offended...'

I am puzzled as to what Michael has to say to me that could possibly cause offence but I encourage him to continue, purely out of curiosity.

'I have been watching you for a while...'

That sounds a bit stalkerish but I guess what with being opposite our stall in the station there isn't much else to look out to other than commuters rushing by.

He pauses for what seems like an eternity and whilst he does so I try to think of all the possible excuses I can tell Tess for my behaviour so far the only one I can think of is that I have a condition called imaginationitis where I just randomly switch off into my own little world and can't do anything about it. Somehow I don't think she is going to buy that excuse.

Michael then clears his throat to continue the conversation.

'....as I just said I've been watching you for a while and I thought it might be nice to go out tonight for a drink or walk along the beach or something. Just as friends of course. What do you say Ruby?'

I look up to the ceiling and silently thank whatever god is up there for letting me off the hook for daydreaming. I don't want to go for a walk with Michael tonight but seeing as he just wants to go as friends and the fact that if I don't accept his offer he may still dob me in I agree to go, despite Tess's warning.

'Sure Michael that would be lovely.'

I couldn't really say no. That will teach me for daydreaming.

'How about when we finish our shifts here we can head towards Bondi Beach' he says ecstatically.

Michael is looking like the cat that got the cream and is grinning from ear to ear after I accept his offer. I am not sure whether to be flattered he seems so keen to spend time with me or a little creeped out.

He takes my hand and says thank you. I've never had anyone thank me before for going on a walk with them. It is a bit odd. Maybe I am so used to dealing with douche bag men that maybe I have forgotten that there are also polite men out there too. Besides it might be good to just go for a walk and see the beach with a guy on platonic terms as it might stop me thinking about Ryan.

After accepting Michael's offer, I feel on edge for the rest of my shift as I can feel his eyes on me the whole time. I am starting to think maybe the wrath of Tess would be a more pleasant experience than a walk with Michael. In fact Tess would probably have given me praise by turning Michael down.

At five o clock on the dot, when the working day had finished, I see that Michael is waiting and watching me silently as I put the last padlock on the shutters of the stall. I wish he would just say something just so this doesn't feel so awkward.

I double check the locks and then walk with Michael to the platform where we get on the crowded train to Bondi Junction. The journey feels like an eternity as I can feel Michael's hot breath on my cheek due to being packed in like sardines on this train. After a moment of breathing space when we get off the train we then get the number 333 bus to the beach, which was even more crowded than the train. The conversation between us is limited due to the heat meaning any sort of movement is an effort. Yet despite the lack of talking Michael's eyes are clearly fixed on me. I don't even think he has blinked once, its rather disconcerting.

I breathe a sigh of relief as the bus finally stops at Bondi Beach and people disembark quickly to get to their final destination. I take a moment to readjust myself after the cramped journey, and then I begin to head to the beachfront with Michael. Even though he is wearing a thick polo neck, he doesn't seem to have dripped a single drop of sweat or look even remotely flustered from the journey. We walk in silence…

…and then I see him.

Of all the people to bump into its him. I am beginning to think this is more than a coincidence now.

He is with a blonde again but this time it is of the male variety instead which is unusual for him so unless his exhausted his ways with women and has moved on to men I am going to presume it is a friend of his.

I have never felt so awkward in my life. I have no idea what to say to him. Although I do feel a slight sense of smugness that he has bumped into me with a male companion, as it gives me a chance to prove I can move on from him even though the reality is I don't really want to be anywhere near Michael right now or at any other time in my life.

'Hiya Ruby. How are ya?'

Even though the question is directed at me, Ryan isn't looking in my direction. Instead he is thoroughly eyeing Michael up and down. I really want to respond back with 'I'm fine, you bastard' but being English and a wuss I decide to be polite.

'Hey Ryan. I am really good thanks. How are you?'

'I'm good. Just heading over to my mate here's barbie to celebrate him turning the big 3-0.'

The blonde guy sticks his hand out for me to shake and I immediately shake his hand back. It feels warm and friendly.

'Hey Ruby, nice to meet ya. My name's Chad by the way. You're more than welcome to join us if you like. There's a few veggies so there will be plenty of snags available unless of course you're bloody veggie too!'

I immediately warm to Chad. He is just like the stereotype laid back Aussie I was expecting most Australians to be like when I arrived here.

I then realise that Michael is standing there like a lemon as I talk to Chad and Ryan. I decide to introduce him to the group in the hope he will like them too and will want to go to the barbecue.

Besides I'd feel less on edge if I wasn't with Michael on my own.

'This is my friend…'

Before I even finish the sentence Michael interrupts and brings the potential barbecue trip to a crashing end.

'Let's hurry along now shall we Ruby, we have a nice walk along the beach to get to, we can't be spending time talking to other men.'

There is an emphasis on the '*other men*'. I didn't realise Michael was the type to view '*other men*' as competition.

He grabs my arm tightly and moves me along as if I am some sort of petulant toddler. I hastily say goodbye to Ryan and Chad and move along. As soon as we are out of earshot of Ryan I tell Michael to ease up a bit.

'Let go of my arm Michael, you are hurting me.'

He loosens his grip a little but he still continues to hold my arm.

'You know I haven't had a girlfriend as pretty as you before. I promised myself that if I ever got to have a girl as pretty as you, I'd make her mine and ensure she'd always be by my side no matter what it takes.'

This is a bit much, I thought we were just going as friends not on a date but even on a first date I wouldn't want to be called someone's 'girlfriend'. I need to get out of this situation. He is really making me feel uncomfortable. In fact I would rather go on another date with the high-pitched weirdo that was Pete than Michael right now.

I try to change the subject and talk to him about the new ice cream shop that has opened up near Bondi Beach and whether it would be worth checking out.

I continue to fill the air with my voice, talking all sorts of crap, in the hope he won't do or say anything else to creep me out. I am hoping he will get so bored he will want to end this date.

We get halfway along the beach and I spot a large square building with a glass balcony, known as North Bondi RSL. That is my target point. Once we get to there I know we can turn back and I can get back home and away from this guy. As I catch my breath from all the talking I have been doing, Michael immediately fills the silence.

'You talk too much. I don't like a girl who talks a lot. Take my hand and let me kiss you on the lips so I can silence you.'

Alarm bells are firing off in all directions inside my brain. This is too full on. I don't want to have any physical contact with him and I do not need to be 'silenced'.

I immediately put both of my hands behind my back so I don't have to touch him although his grip on my left arm is getting tighter.

'Are you deaf? I said take my hand.'

He is getting more and more aggressive and I don't know what to do. His grip is so tight my arm now feels numb but I still refuse to take his hand or get anywhere near his lips despite his attempts to try and move his head closer to mine.

After several attempts of ducking and diving he finally lets go of my arm but then he begins to hurl a fury of angry words in my direction.

'You will pay for this you fucking bitch. You pretty girls are all the same, you use and abuse guys like me and then go off with some other guy who is better looking or has more money...'

I try desperately to think of something to calm the situation and to prevent him getting angrier.

'No Michael, I am not like that. I want to be your friend.'

'My friend!' he viciously spits out from his mouth. 'You're not my friend you are just some attention seeking whore.'

I feel physically sick and my adrenaline is sky high. The more I try to pacify Michael the angrier he seems to be getting.

He reaches into his pocket and pulls out something in his hand that is metallic. I try to breathe in and out slowly and hope it isn't what I think it is.

CHAPTER 20

Chad turns thirty today. Being three years younger I like to rip the shit out of him for it by calling him Grandpa Chad and telling him it won't be long until he collects his superannuation but as usual with Chad he just takes it all in his stride and ignores all the comments. It's a shame his girlfriend doesn't do the same.

I remember when I was about thirteen years old and me asking Chad what he thought our lives would be like when we were thirty and to this day his answer still makes me laugh. He said that when he was thirty he hoped to be the richest beach bum in the world ever.

I on the other hand said I wanted a job in the city, a super-fast red sports car and a sexy blonde chick to be my wife who I can go on fancy holidays to Brisbane with.

Well I pretty much nailed the first thing on my list with a job as a senior accountant in one of the top accountancy firms in the city, although still eyeing up being a partner. Just got to wait for old Gerry to kick the bucket and the post should be mine. I do drive a red car, however it's a Holden not a Ferrari so not quite the sports car I was hoping for. I don't have a sexy wife to share my adventures with but who needs one woman to have fun with when you can have multiple to pick up and put down when I choose. Okay who am I kidding…I secretly would love a sexy blonde wife as my companion as after these past couple of weeks of chasing after girls and getting a quick lay are getting a bit boring. I need someone who is able to hold a decent conversation not someone who looks decent holding a cocktail but can't string a sentence together.

Although I daren't let Chad know my change in heart about relationships otherwise it'll be his turn to rip the shit out of me.

And as far as fancy holidays to Brisbane go, I've also realised that whilst it is an okay city I wouldn't put it as the most exotic of places to head to.

I may not have reached all my goals yet but I feel pretty okay with what I have achieved so far.

Chad on the other hand has pretty much nailed the beach bum vibe to a tee but seeing as he works as a baker I don't think he has made it as the most minted beach bum in the world.

Although Chad hasn't reached his goal, he doesn't seem too fussed about getting older or what life has ahead for him, he just takes every day as it comes. To him every day is a new adventure.

His main priority seems to be catching the 'gnarliest of waves' and having an awesome time whilst doing so. In a way I quite like his simple way of looking at the world. He'd probably be a good psychology subject for my parents to look in to as I've never come across any one so chilled as him.

'Yo, ground control to Ryan, is anybody in there?' shouts Chad right in front of my face.

Looks like I have been caught daydreaming. I've never done that in front of Chad before, I feel rather sheepish and snap out of my thoughts immediately.

'Sorry Dude. What were you saying?'

'For a moment there, I thought you were spaced out on drugs or something, anyway never mind dude. What I was trying to say was did we remember to get some veggie sausages and burgers for Charlie because if we don't, we need to go back as I do not want my ears to be subject to a whole load of verbal abuse on my birthday. All I want is peace, harmony, beers and burgers.'

I let out a small smile and we place the carrier bags full of goods on the pavement to have a look. As we stop to look in the plastic bag to check we have Charlie's food I get distracted by a couple walking towards us.

This is the third time we've spontaneously bumped into each other like this. I'm almost wondering if this is a sign. My heart is hammering big time in my chest but I try my best to remain composed.

'Hey Ruby, how are ya?'

She responds with a generic, 'I'm really good' answer that most girls will do as if they are trying to play it cool but the reality is that they are pissed off with you. Not surprising really when I never got back in contact with her.

I decide to introduce Chad to her as every girl that has met Chad warms to him instantly. This might also soften the blow for me and show that I do have friends of the male variety not just female. It's funny though, Chad just has to smile at girls and they fall for his charms yet he stays as faithful to Charlie like an obedient golden retriever despite all the goodies available to him.

I see Ruby's shoulders relax as soon as Chad starts talking to her and it is clear the Chad charm is working its magic. He's even asked her to his birthday barbecue. Good move Chad. Somehow I wonder if his sub-consciously picked up the vibe that I am into this chick.

I notice Ruby's eyes light up and I immediately get the butterflies in my stomach feeling as she looks like she is going to say yes. I feel excited that I might get another chance with her and also nervous that I might end up fucking this up again and lose the chance forever to make her my girlfriend. That's right, I said the word 'girlfriend', after meeting Ruby my thoughts on 'relationships' have definitely taken a U-turn.

Just as Ruby is about to respond, the Dementor that is stuck on to her arm decides to ruin the whole situation by moving Ruby along meaning our conversation has come to an end and that my chance to make amends has gone out of the water again.

I secretly hope that the guy gets a whole load of sand in his eyes and that Ruby finds him a complete bore and would want to give me a second chance. This is unlikely though as this stuff only happens in the movies not real life.

Although I really didn't like the way that guy was grabbing her arm, it just didn't look right.

I start to look back in the bags we have to see whether we have Charlie's veggie stuff but Chad brushes my hand away;

'Don't worry about the veggie stuff, I checked whilst you were drooling over that girl.'

'I was not drooling Chad, she is just a friend.'

'Friend my ass dude. So are you going to tell me about this chick then?'

I tell Chad the whole story as to how we met and the dates we'd been on. I never really go into any detail with the girls I have dated with Chad but somehow I feel the need to tell him everything about Ruby. I've always trusted Chad and whenever I have an issue I just open up like a double click. My mother always says that when it comes to emotions it's always better to be out than in, although I thought that was more to do with farts than emotions but who am I to argue when she's sold 1.3 million books on how to find that perfect relationship.

'Maaaaatteeee sounds like you have been hit by the love train hard.'

'I don't think so Chad, this guy is still on the lust carriage and he has no signs of getting off anytime soon.' I reply. Although I secretly know he is right.

'Whatever Dude'. He knows that I am giving a bullshit response back but also knows not to push the topic any further. We then continue the rest of the walk to the flat in silence with just the sound of our thongs pounding the pavement and the rustle of plastic bags.

During the period of silence I begin reminiscing to myself about the dates I had been on with Ruby and the fun we had. I still have the picture she drew of the hotel in my wallet. When we get to Chad's flat, he begins to fumble around for his keys and as he does so I decide to take the opportunity to get a sneak peak of the drawing. As I pull it out of my wallet I feel my heart beat become unusually fast again. I unfold it and look at all the detailed pencil etchings and I smile a small smile to myself.

An idea then flashes in my brain. Chad's girlfriend Charlie is an editor for an arts and craft magazine, I might see if she wants to publish Ruby's drawing as she is always moaning that she can't find an illustrator.

'Dude. Why are you staring into space again, I'm going to start getting you to pay me ten dollars every time you do that. Come inside. And what's that piece of paper in your hand?'

Woah Chad seems to be in a bit of a mood this evening, ninety nine per cent of the time he is a chilled out dude so something must have rattled his cage. It probably doesn't help when I've been daydreaming most of the journey to the flat.

'Sorry dude, just thinking about stuff. Is Charlie in by the way?'

'No worries. Let's put these beers in the fridge ey and we can have a few coldies in half an hour. And yes of course Charlie is in, she's the one who organised my birthday BBQ so don't start causing an argument with her.'

'I can hear my name' says a voice from the stairs.

'Hey Charlie' I muster in my best fake friendly voice.

'Look Ryan, if you are going to be rude. I suggest that you get it out of your system now so we can try and have a nice evening for Chad's birthday.'

'Look I am sorry I've pissed you off in the past Charlie and I promise I'll be on my best behaviour tonight. Besides I have something that may be of interest to you.'

'Yeah right Ryan, what do you have that will be of interest to me?'

I show her the piece of paper.

'I know you are always looking for art work to go in your magazine. Just wondered if this would be of interest to you?'

I see her eyes widen and I know I have definitely piqued her interest and so it should it's one of the best drawings I have ever seen.

'Did you do this? It's really quite something.'

I burst out laughing and shake my head side to side to confirm that it was not me who drew such a masterpiece. I may be able to draw up a budget but I certainly can't draw anything remotely artistic.

I quickly remove the smile from my face and go back to poker mode as Charlie looks like she might get angry again due to my response and I don't want to ruin this chance for Ruby.

'It's drawn by someone of the name Ruby Samuels.'

'Well as far as I am aware you don't have any relatives of that name, so I am going to deduce that it's from a lady friend of yours. You must clearly like her though as I've never seen you go out of your way for a girl before like this. I'm not sure whether I am more surprised over the picture or the fact you might actually have feelings for a girl.'

'Shut up Charlie. It's none of your business whether I like her or have feelings for her. Do you want to publish the picture or not?'

'Woah, you are seriously touchy this evening! And yes, I will publish the drawing, it is really beautiful, I haven't seen such good artwork like this in a long while. I may need to contact her for more illustrations if it works well in this magazine, if you don't mind.'

I pass on Ruby's details to her and feel secretly pleased on behalf of Ruby that Charlie is going to publish her drawing. I immediately start thinking of all the ways I can surprise her and take her out for dinner but as I do so the images in my head of surprising Ruby get ruined by that guy who was holding her arm tightly and giving me the evilest of stares. My gut instinct tells me something doesn't feel right between her and that guy and I need to go and investigate further. I immediately allay my fears to Chad.

'I don't know what it is but that guy with Ruby just looked a bit shifty. He seemed to be holding on to her arm a little bit too tightly for my liking. Do you fancy going for a walk along the beach? Just to check that everything is okay.'

'Oh come on Dude, I've only just sat down and opened a cold one. Do you really think it's a good idea to gate crash their date tonight? You'll look a right Desperate Dan.'

'I'm not desperate. I just have this odd feeling that something isn't right. I see no harm in just walking by to check everything is okay and maybe let her know about the drawing Charlie is going to publish and that she might want to get in contact.'

Okay now I am starting to sound like some whiney tosser by thinking of all the excuses possible to see Ruby again, although I really don't feel right about her with that guy, unless as much as I hate to admit it I actually feel jealous of them on a date but why would I feel jealous of a guy who wears a turtle neck?

No something isn't right about him other than his dire fashion sense.

I really want to see her and I really want to see her now.

'Dude you really do have the hots for her and you know what, good. It's about time you connected with your feelings and experience a bit of love in your life. Lusting does you no good except landing you with nasty diseases.'

'Okay I'll admit that I have a soft spot for the girl but as to lusting it's perfectly healthy and I let you know I always use protection so have remained disease free thank you very much. So are you walking or not?'

'Sure whatever Dude. You know I can't resist a walk by the ocean to see the waves, although if Charlie sees us going for a walk together she will think we are conspiring against her or some sort of shit like that. You go on ahead and I'll catch up. Besides I need to choke down... I mean chew one of these veggie burgers first.'

One thing is for sure I would not be pretending to be a veggie for any girl no matter how hot she is. I really don't understand why Chad puts all that effort in for a miserable cow like Charlie. At least Ruby knows how to smile.

Ah Ruby, she's infected my brain but in a weird way I like it. Then the image of that creep she was with earlier clouds my happy thoughts again. I make my exit from the barbecue and hope that the date Ruby is on is going terrible but not so bad the guy is making her cry her eyes out.

After a few minutes' walk from Chad's place I hit the Bondi seafront. It's dusk now so the light is starting to fade meaning the beach is near enough deserted. It's funny I've never really paid much attention to Bondi beach despite growing up so close to it. It's weird to think that this small strip of sand is the number one spot for tourists when there are so many other beautiful beaches along the New South Wales coast. I suppose it has its charm due to the good restaurants nearby and the yellow soft sand. It is also a prime spot to pick up some horny tourists but for a change I am not interested in finding one to shack up with as there's only one girl I want to find this evening.

I notice two figures further up the beach and immediately recognise Ruby's wavy blonde hair. He seems to be making a move, I feel a sinking feeling in my stomach as this guy will get to touch Ruby's beautiful and delicate skin. Although she seems to have brushed off his advances and my insides lift slightly.

Suddenly things take a turn for the worse. It's worse than I could have ever have imagined. He begins pushing and shoving her about into the sand and as Ruby tries to straighten up he begins to pull something out of his pocket.

The guy has a knife.

Instinct kicks in and I run as fast as my legs can take me to get to Ruby and this psycho in order to prevent her being injured.

Please don't hurt her. Please. She is such an innocent and beautiful human being, she does not deserve this.

I shout at the top of my lungs 'RUBY I'M COMING…GET AWAY FROM HER YOU BASTARD!'

It's too late he has stabbed her in the arm. I see him pin her to the ground. I continue to shout at him and push sand in his direction. He eventually turns around to face me and as I get face to face with him I pull him off Ruby whilst at the same time managing to get a strong grip on his knife arm. Even though his other arm is taking swipes at my body in order to take me out, I continue to tighten my grip on his knife arm and eventually he drops the blade to the ground. I use my foot to kick it away and get a blast full of sand in my eyes in the process but at least he cannot hurt Ruby anymore.

I then twist his arm around his back and use my other arm to continue to punch the sack of shit until he is on the ground and unable to move. If I could get away with it, I would've killed the guy.

As I see that the guy will not be getting up from the ground anytime soon, I hear Chad's voice behind me and several people running out of the nearby restaurants and shops who have obviously seen and heard the commotion.

'Dude what the fuck?!'

I sweep Ruby up in my arms, the colour of her clothes begins to reflect the colour of her name as blood begins to pour down my shirt. I hold her closer to my chest in the hope it will make things better and stop the blood seeping from her arm.

I tell her she is safe and I see a faint smile across her lips.

I take a deep breath to remain calm and respond back to Chad;

'Call an ambulance Chad. We need to get her to the hospital.'

I hear her croak out my name and then her eyes shut and her head falls to the side as flashing sirens come closer to us.

Please don't let this be the end.

CHAPTER 21

'Ryan, is that you?'

I feel his strong and comforting arms around my body. I am too weak to respond any further. I don't know what is happening to me. I can just about make out a muffled sound of sirens, then the world became silent and black.

CHAPTER 22

Swoosh. I push my body deep into the water of the Bondi Icebergs swimming pool in the hope that it provides some calmness to all the thoughts exploding in my head. But it doesn't, with each stroke flashbacks from the incident fill my mind.

Ruby laid so silently and still at the back of the ambulance. I held her hand the whole way, desperate not to lose her. Yet, as soon as we got to the hospital my hand just let go and she was whisked away to be treated on her own.

I couldn't stay. I felt out of place as I wasn't her next of kin or even her boyfriend. I felt so helpless. I couldn't sleep the rest of the night as I was constantly thinking what if. What if I just stayed with her at the hospital? What if I followed through my feelings for her that night at the Harbour? How could I have left Ruby like that?

I try and direct all my energy into pushing and pulling each of my strokes in and out of the water to try and block out the outside world.

The water is where I feel safest. Just me and the water. No need to worry about love and what happened to Ruby here.

Oh Ruby….

After forty five minutes of pounding the water my lungs begin to struggle and my arms and legs feel like jelly so I decide to call it a day. Besides the chattering voices in my head have quietened as I know what action I need to take to prevent anything like last night happening again.

I begin to pull myself out of the pool and get ready to put my plan into action but before I do so an overweight man in budgie smugglers, whose lack of hair on his head was made up by the amount on his chest, decides to get in my way.

'Been seeing you thrash that water mate…are you a relation of Thorpedo or something as I've never seen anyone in this pool hit the water like you just did. You'll have to join the swimming club here mate, will probably do a lonely sod like you some good.'

I pray he doesn't want to chat any longer as I don't need this right now. I have something important to do. I feel like telling him to go do one and that a fat bastard like him should go and join the local slimmers club as it would probably do him some good too.

Instead I just smile and begin making my way swiftly to the changing room.

Luckily the smile was enough as he waddles off in his speedos towards the shallow end of the pool meaning I can get out of here pronto.

I then notice the lifeguard on duty is checking me out. She doesn't look any older than twenty with wavy caramel hair and a button shaped nose, usually I'd be responding back with some flirty vibes but this time I don't even bother catching her eye and carrying on to the changing room.

God what is it with people today, the day I need to get somewhere I have every obstacle in my way before I get to do it.

I quickly shower, dry and change back into my clothes. This is it. No turning back and no more distractions, it's time to go back to the hospital and visit Ruby.

CHAPTER 23

Visiting Sydney Hospital was definitely not on my bucket list when visiting Australia. Yet here I am sitting in a hospital bed with stitches in my left arm, trying to work out what an earth happened last night. I try to piece together what happened but I can't as every time I try to picture the scenario I get Maureen in the bed opposite me shouting out random crossword clues in the hope that someone on the ward will be able to help her out. Despite the silence she continues to read the clues aloud.

'6 letters, begins with I, a reptile creature...ooh I think I know this one...now it's not lizard'

Clearly one of the patients has had enough of Maureen's outbursts and shouts back at her;

'It's Iguana now put a sock in it you dumb old bat before I ask the nurse to give you another bed bath.'

I put a hand over my mouth to prevent myself from laughing out loud. I see Maureen's face get red with embarrassment and she then tosses her crossword book across the floor.

A few moments after Maureen's rage at the crossword book, I see out of the corner of my eye two pairs of legs walking towards me and as they get closer I realise that it is Martha and Chloe.

Simultaneously I feel a sense of relief but also a sense of guilt that I have ended up in this position and my sister has to see me in hospital like this.

Martha looked as my mother would say 'white as a sheet'. I know she is hurting as much as I am. I remember when Martha broke her leg on a school trip to Snowdonia rock climbing. I had this feeling of cramp in my left leg right up until the day she had her cast off. We may be different but there is always a connection between us.

Martha's eyes are panic stricken and as she gets to my bed she begins to talk hurriedly.

'The hospital didn't phone until this morning otherwise I would have come sooner. I just presumed you got lucky on one of your GirlmeetsBoy dates. I am so so sorry Ruby. I let you down, if I wasn't so involved with my own life I would be able to spend more time with you and you wouldn't be in this position and you wouldn't end up…with a…. with a…scar.'

'At least people will be able to tell us apart' I jest light-heartedly.

Yet rather than the usual Martha response of a laugh or follow up joke she just burst into tears and I end up doing the same.

An authoritative Spanish voice prevents us from becoming even more of a jibbering wreck.

'Will the pair of you stop crying, you'll make me cry and I've only just put eyeliner on an hour ago.'

We both then change from tears of sadness to tears of laughter at Chloe and then we realise she was actually being serious with the eyeliner comment which makes us laugh even more. She ignores our laughing at her and continues talking;

'The nurse told us you should be out in a few hours so when you return to the flat I want to treat you to a special Spanish food feast. You girls will be swapping those tears of pain for tears of joy as I make the best Paella in Barcelona! It will be Caspita!'

I have no idea what 'Caspita' means but my stomach grumbles at the thought of food and I realise its been a while since I've had something to eat as I skipped the hospital breakfast as soggy toast with marmalade made me feel queasy.

Martha then makes herself comfortable on my bed, even when we were younger she always liked to nestle into my space but this time I don't object to her pushing me up against the side of the bed as it makes me feel secure and comfortable. Chloe however decides to stand like a majestic horse, proud and strong but despite appearances we sat and talked for two solid hours as if nothing had really happened and we were back in our flat rather than a hospital ward.

Martha and Chloe also helped Maureen with her crossword which was a relief to both me and the rest of the members of the ward. In fact Chloe is quite a whizz at these things despite being Spanish, as she used them as a way to learn different words in the English language.

With only ten minutes to go before visiting time was over it was time for Martha and Chloe to go, they insisted they wanted to stay and wait until I was discharged but to be honest I just wanted a few minutes of breathing space to myself to think about last night and to process what has happened.

I promised Martha I would ring her when I was out and that I would get a taxi back. It's funny we both promised ourselves we wouldn't end up like our mother yet here Martha is, acting just like her.

Just as Martha and Chloe leave through the exit door I hear a familiar voice come through the entrance door at the other end.

It's Ryan. It's fucking Ryan.

As he looks to the left of the wall I manage to slide back down under my sheets and close my eyes to make it look as if I have been asleep for a few hours.

My heart is going so fast I begin to wonder whether it will burst out of my chest. If it wasn't for Ryan I would probably be lying in a morgue rather than a hospital bed, I cannot thank him enough. Yet at the same time I wish it wasn't him who saved me as I had just got to a stage where I thought I was over pining for him but after last night and the way he held me tightly and spoke so tenderly. I felt as if he was the One again. His was the last face I remembered before I ended up here but I didn't expect to see his face again.

I wonder what he is doing here? Maybe he just feels the need to check up on me as a friend or something. Or maybe he isn't visiting me at all, maybe he is actually here to see Maureen, she might be his aunt twice removed or something and is just paying her a friendly visit.

The suspense is killing me, yet I don't dare open my eyes. I breathe in more deeply to control my breathing and begin to count to ten. If I don't hear anything after ten I will slowly open my eyes as if nothing has happened.

One…two…Jesus Christ!!

I feel a touch of someone's hand on my hand and my eyes fling wide open. I see that it is Ryan and that he is trying to hold my hand, confirming that he isn't some estranged nephew of Maureen he really has come to see me.

I try to sit up and put on a seductive voice to say hello and all that comes out is a voice that sounds like a ninety year old woman who smokes ten packs of cigarettes a day. I blame all the talking to Chloe and Martha and lack of water. As soon as the thought of water comes to my head I see that Ryan is already putting a glass to my lips and placing his hand on my back to help support me.

I really wasn't expecting this. It's almost as if someone has packed the Ryan who lusts after every lady in a box and brought out the caring and considerate Ryan instead. I am beginning to wonder whether he got concussion when he got into that fight with Michael.

I am quite taken aback by it all. I also secretly hope this really is my chance for a shot at something more with Ryan. And then I remember my scar, why would anyone be interested in someone with a hulking great red mark down their arm, especially Ryan with his access to any bevy of beauties.

I see him looking at the scar. I immediately want to cry but instead I blurt out about how ugly the scar is to him.

The response he gave in return shocked me, in fact it shocked me so much I began to tear up. He didn't view it as something ugly but rather something beautiful instead. If I could marry this man now I would, even if it meant Maureen was our only witness. For a few moments we look intently into each other's eyes and I feel that there really is a connection between us that I had never felt with someone before.

He then reaches for something in his back pocket. By the looks of things it's an arts magazine, wouldn't have thought it was his cup of tea but he is looking at the pages studiously as he flicks through it.

How bloody rude! We have this connection and his response is to ignore it and start reading a magazine. Well so much for Ryan changing into a new and improved gentleman. Just at the moment where I was going to tell him to leave and that he should head to the library if he wants to go and read, he then places the magazine on my lap. The picture I see in front of me nearly makes me press the buzzer for the nurse in case I have a cardiac arrest.

It's my drawing.

One of my drawings is in a magazine. It's published with my name on it. How did it end up here? Then it dawned on me. When I thought I had left the drawing at the hotel by accident, I clearly didn't, Ryan must have taken it. I feel like I should be seriously angry with him for taking a picture that was personal to me but I don't. He has helped me get one step closer to my dream of being an illustrator. I am silent from the shock, which seems to unnerve Ryan slightly as he begins to change the topic of conversation.

'I've bought you some flowers too. I stopped off at the train station on the way and got Tess to wrap them up especially.'

Okay now this guy has really pulled out all the stops. I just can't believe this is all happening at once. Last night I thought my world had ended and now I feel like I am top of the world.

I compose myself from my flabbergasted state and thank Ryan from the bottom of my heart for getting my drawing into a magazine, although I did give him a bit of stick for not asking my permission first.

I notice his shoulders begin to relax once I confirm that I am over the moon about the drawing and not angry about it at all. He then proceeds to tell me how he got it published and that there is a chance the magazine will want more of my pictures. I start to take long deep breaths as this can't be real. Maybe I'm still unconscious and this is all a dream.

After the talk about the magazine the conversation comes to an end all I think about is wanting to kiss him. This may take my head out of the clouds and crashing down to reality but I don't feel I can pass this opportunity up to have one more final shot with Ryan. I move closer to him and his beautiful lips and he seems to be moving closer too, our lips are almost at touching point and then...

Whoosh...

I hear the sound of the curtains round one side of my bed get pushed and a bellowing voice fills the ward. Looks like I won't be getting any kisses from Ryan, instead it looks like I will get whippings from the nurse for getting up to no good. I feel so embarrassed and just want to hide under the bed sheets again.

Ryan also looks equally embarrassed as he is bearing the brunt of a firm chastisement from the nurse for our bedside activities. This woman clearly does not take any messing about, in fact she looks exactly like Mrs Trunchbull from the book *Matilda*.

She then ignores Ryan and tends to me in order that she carry out her checks and hopefully I can be discharged and leave this place. Despite being told to leave Ryan is still standing at the end of the bed.

The nurse notices this too and shouts at him again but he seems frozen to the spot.

It looks like Ryan may have finally met his match with this feisty woman as she certainly has put him in his place. I wonder whether I should just watch this play out a little bit longer for my own amusement but I think better of it and tell Ryan to meet me in the cafe. I also gently suggest to him that I would like some doughnuts as I have a real hankering for them.

Although I really do hope he gets them for me as I am positively starving right now. Maybe I can lick the sugar off his lips as an added bonus too…. oooh those are some naughty thoughts. Thank goodness I didn't say them out loud as this nurse is seriously not in the mood for any funny business. Her face and attitude remain firm and she is vigorously ticking off the items on her clipboard ready for me to be discharged. She's poked my arm about fifteen times already to check that the stitches will hold. Although fifteen times it has been confirmed I am not in a dream, Ryan really did come to see me and hopefully in five minutes, once Mrs Trunchbull has finished poking and prodding my arm and every other body part, I will get to see him again.

CHAPTER 24

My leg is going up and down faster than a merry go round. I put my hand on my leg to stop myself but I can't. I think the last time I was this nervous was at my interview for my first accountant job at Charter and Charter. I somehow, despite the nerves managed to ace the interview and secure my dream job, so I am hoping, by the luck of the gods I can secure my dream girl.

God I am so on edge, I've already been to the toilet five times, nervous shits are not what I want right now. The fact I have ordered us chocolate doughnuts as well as jam doughnuts doesn't help the situation either.

I suddenly see Ruby walking across the café towards me. I wave at her and also push my sphincter tighter in the hope that I can prevent soiling my pants in front of this beautiful woman.

I don't know whether to get up and give her a kiss on the cheek as a greeting or smile and show her her seat, but as I am riddled with nerves I end up doing neither and instead sit there like an invalid. I probably fit in with the rest of this crowd in the hospital cafe, but it probably doesn't make the best impressions with Ruby.

Although she appears unconcerned about my lack of greetings as she sits down in the chair opposite me and goes straight in with a challenge of getting me to eat one of the sugary jam doughnuts on the table in front of us without licking my lips.

I am taken aback by her approach but in a way I am relieved. Besides if I have a face full of doughnut it means that I won't need to start the conversation. Ruby will have to take the lead and it will take the pressure of me and my bowels for a moment.

I take a big bite of the doughnut and as I do so, Ruby then decides to stick her tongue in and out of her mouth like some demented chameleon.

Her lizard act almost makes me choke on my doughnut as it makes me laugh out loud, I know she is deliberately trying to get me to lose and I do my best to keep my composure but I just can't and it involuntary makes my tongue say hello to the world.

'You lose!' she shouts as her shoulders shake up and down with laughter.

I try to feign denial, but it is pretty clear I failed and do you know what I don't care and by the looks of things Ruby doesn't either.

This is what I love about Ruby, she isn't afraid to make a fool of herself and she is just so genuine. There is no false persona or the need to always be the best, she is just…just her.

I decide to tell her my true feelings towards her. Although her response is to brush the compliments under the carpet.

'That's all very well and good, but you still lost the doughnut challenge.'

I grab her hand to show that I want to have a serious conversation with her. I also need something to hold on to in order to calm my nerves.

I have never been so honest with a girl before.

'You are beautiful inside and out…I promise I will protect you…'

I await Ruby's reaction and hope that at least she sees me as a friend. Although to be this honest with her has been a relief.

Ruby sits there dumbfounded without saying a word.

I can't stand the tension between us any longer so I decided to crack a joke about not wanting another date at this café. She laughs softly and says that she does not want a return trip here either. She then looks up at the clock on the wall and tells me she has to leave.

It's like she has punched me in the stomach. God I am such an idiot. If I just kept my mouth shut about telling her how beautiful she was until after a few more meet ups, she probably wouldn't be trying to run away as fast as she is now.

Why does everything with women have to be so complicated? I'm starting to wonder whether Ruby has been reading my mother's books…. I bloody hope not as I have enough trouble dealing with mother let alone having to deal with a potential junior version of her.

I've just compared a girl I like to my mother...Christ I really am losing the plot.

Ruby then stops my spinning head in its tracks as she asks me the question I was dying to hear;

'So are you free tomorrow for a date? That's if you want to go for a date that is.'

Wow. I can't believe it. I almost want to do a Tom Cruise and jump on the table but I think better of it as it might scare Ruby off and besides I'd probably get that nurse come over and sedate me or flip me upside down and use me as a mop or something…that nurse is not a woman I ever want to come across again.

I give Ruby a clear yes and that she should get ready to have her 'mind-blown' for the date I am going to organise for us. I immediately cringe at the use of the phrase 'mind-blown' but she seemed to laugh and says she 'can't wait to see what I have planned for her'.

We part ways with a hug, which was a bit awkward due to her sore arm but still I AM GOING ON A DATE WITH RUBY!!

As I head back to my flat, I can hear my bowels gurgling again as the pressure is on to create a 'mind-blowing' date tomorrow. I better think of something pretty damn cool to do near Sydney Harbour otherwise I probably won't have another chance of making this work with Ruby. I think I might need to consult my friend Google on this one and hope he comes up with something decent.

*   *   *

After returning to the flat and spending another thirty minutes on the toilet seat, I began to do some thinking about our date tomorrow, not sure why but toilets are always the best place to think up ideas if you are a man. Aristotle probably came up with his best theories whilst taking a dump, although I doubt any history book will confirm it as it doesn't sound quite as fancy as coming up with ideas in a botanical garden or temple.

Anyway, whilst thinking of things we can do, it suddenly dawned on me that our last date was at Sydney Harbour so we should head back there. I can't stand Opera so that rules out the Opera House. Although there is the Bridge…yes the bridge will be excellent. I will book us on a sunset climb. It will be romantic and adventurous. All sorted.

Oh shit…I've run out of toilet roll.

CHAPTER 25

Well Ryan really did give me a date to remember and no I don't mean we got down and dirty. Instead we went up and got flighty. Well I felt a bit flighty, Ryan seemed to be cooler than an ice cube.

Ryan clearly decided that being attacked on a beach hadn't raised my adrenaline quite high enough, as he decided our date should consist of us climbing Sydney Harbour Bridge at sunset. Quite frankly I would've been happy just to have had a look at the bridge from the harbour at sunset and seen that as a pretty awesome date but Ryan had other ideas. Just looking up at the bridge makes me feel queasy.

I couldn't say no as he had this puppy dog look which you just don't want to upset and he'd greeted me with the biggest bunch of pink damask roses I have ever seen. They were just beautiful, they are my favourite flowers too. He clearly had done his homework with Tess and I would feel terrible for ruining the plans for our first date after the accident so I agreed to climb the bridge. When I said yes he kissed me gently on the forehead and slipped his hand in mine.

I gave him a squeeze of his hand to show that I was happy to go along with his date idea. Although my brain was screaming the opposite and that I am going to die.

When we got to the climb centre, we put on these grey jumpsuits on which made me feel like a sack of potatoes...so much for trying to be a glamour puss on this date, although Ryan looked rather handsome in his.

They then gave us the usual safety talk and by that time I really was thinking I was going to die yet somehow I managed to make my way to the beginning of the bridge and the climb and latch myself on to the railings on the side, just a piece of material stopping me from plunging into the harbour below.

Despite my legs feeling like mush and being accompanied by the taste of sick continually rising in my throat, we made it to the top of the bridge and although at times I was feeling like a human washing machine from all the worrying I was doing, the view made the exhausting and nerve wracking journey worthwhile and surprisingly on the way back down to the ground I began to enjoy myself a little especially as it meant I had a full view of Ryan's bum as he sashayed down the steps.

And as an added bonus I didn't die which meant that I could enjoy a deep and satisfying kiss from Ryan and an ice cream for being a 'brave girl'. Ryan can be such a sarcastic sod sometimes. I knew he knew I was nervous but in a way the sarcasm, the fun and the nerves were all just part of the adventure of this new relationship we are embarking on together. I can't wait to organise the next adventurous date.

CHAPTER 26

The past few weeks have just been a whirlwind of amazing dates, with my girlfriend, Ruby. That's right I called her my girlfriend. The bachelor life is now just a distant memory, although I thought I might have blown my chances with the Bridge date. It probably wasn't the best idea to do something quite as adventurous as a climb with Ruby considering what she had recently gone through. Yet despite her initial nervousness, she went with the idea and seemed to enjoy it by the end. Whether her mind was blown is a different question, although I think I got pretty close.

The look on her face at the top of the bridge was priceless. She was in such awe of the sunset and the view of Sydney and to be fair so was I. It's a beautiful city and now I get to enjoy it with a beautiful girl.

Today's date has been organised by Ruby, which is to hang out on Bondi beach. I wasn't sure whether that was a good idea due to what happened last time but Ruby was pretty determined that we should go as she wanted to make new and happy memories there.

Even though we are just going to the beach I am still getting stressed out about what to wear.

Red or blue. Red or blue. I really can't decide. Red might make me look a bit like a David Hasselhoff wannabe so maybe I'll go with the blue. In the past I wouldn't give a flying fandango what pair of trunks I wore as long as they fitted but now with Ruby on the scene I want to do my upmost to make the right impression, especially as I feel today might be the day to invite her back to mine.

Oh shit, its 2:10pm, I was meant to meet Ruby at Bondi beach at 2pm. I quickly pull on my blue swimmers and t-shirt and head out of the door.

CHAPTER 27

'Follow your heart' were Tess's parting words to me after I did my last shift at 'Fascinating Florals'. And right now I feel I am doing exactly that and it feels amazing, well other than the part where I am currently getting sand in my eyes waiting for Ryan to turn up at Bondi Beach.

In the weeks that followed our Bridge date we have spent so much time together. I can now tick off the bucket list that I have seen an opera despite Ryan's initial reluctance, I have fed giraffes at Taronga Zoo and know how to say a few words in Italian thanks to a few visits to Gino's restaurant. And the best thing is I've been able to share these special moments with Ryan.

Although all this eating out is starting to make me into a bit of a chunky monkey, somewhere between seeing Ryan, dreaming about Ryan and illustrating I will have to fit in some exercise to work off all this rich and indulgent food I have been eating recently. Thankfully my swimsuit still fits at the moment.

I've also met up with Chad and Charlie who are just awesome. They both have that laid-back, hippy vibe which immediately puts you at ease. Even though Charlie is technically my boss we get on like a house on fire discussing creative ideas and sharing recipes for fruit smoothies.

Since Ryan gave Charlie my sketch of the hotel lobby I have had a flurry of magazine editors wanting to commission me for my work. I can't quite believe it, after all this time struggling with my art and thinking it is not good enough for anyone to see, I seem to have made a break through as not only is my work being published I am getting paid for it too. It did mean however, that I had to give up my job at 'Fascinating Florals.'

Although to be honest, ever since the incident with Michael I hadn't been that keen to go back to work there. Michael was found guilty two weeks ago of my assault. Apparently, I wasn't the only girl he attacked but thankfully he is now serving a lengthy prison sentence.

Tess was so kind to me when I came to see her at the stall. She immediately put her arms around me and gave me a big hug. I told her she was my 'fairy godmother' as without her I don't think I would've lasted that long in the city what with her giving me a job at the stall and giving me the odd motherly advice such as 'are you eating enough Ruby?' and 'make sure you look after yourself'. During my absence, Chloe has stepped in as she unfortunately lost the job at the cafe she was working in, although having a blazing row with the manager as to how to make 'authentic paella' probably didn't help her situation. I just hope she isn't this fiery with Tess or my sister.

Everything seems to be going so well lately, it is almost too good to be true.

My scar is healing nicely which means I can finally go swimming in the ocean. I chose Bondi as the place to swim as I feel it is the right time to move on and make good memories with Ryan here.

I've always loved the ocean. The sounds of the waves crashing on the shore and the feel of the grainy wet sand sinking between my toes. It is one of the few places which makes me feel calm and myself.

As I enjoy the sea breeze on my skin I hear a voice which melts my heart;

'Sorry I'm late I was just having a quick catch-up with Chad on the phone and lost track of the time'.

'Well it looks like we will have to make up for lost time by going straight in the sea…On your marks get set go….'

Before Ryan even has a chance to change his mind I am already running towards the ocean, leaving my shorts and shirt behind on the sand and revealing my red swimsuit to the beach. As I look behind I see that he has decided to follow me and I begin to giggle as I plunge straight into the water.

I feel the coolness of the water lap at my legs and then I see Ryan just inches behind me. I look at him straight in the eyes and as he does so he leans closer for a kiss. In response I throw myself in the water and begin to swim away.

'Catch me if you can' I shout.

He grins and dives straight in the water to catch up. After just a few strokes he is already level with me. He then moves back half a stroke and then gently grabs hold of one of my legs.

'Caught you!' he shouts back at me. I twist my body round in the water to face him and stick out my tongue. He then pulls my leg closer to him so I am within touching distance again, he lets go of my leg and in return I give him a salty and satisfying kiss.

We spent what felt like several hours in the sea, swimming,

attempting to dive to the bottom and splashing each other as if we were kids again. Not only were my arms and legs beginning to tire but my face as well due to all the smiling I have done today.

We eventually make it back to the shore where after drying myself off and applying factor gazillion on my body…with a little help from Ryan of course, I take a moment to admire Ryan's toned and tanned body. He looks so at ease in himself as he lays down on his towel soaking up the afternoon sun rays.

He catches me looking at him.

'What?' he says suspiciously.

'Oh nothing, I'm just admiring the view'.

He rolls his eyes and I swear I see his cheeks turn a slightly pink colour. He then changes the topic and decides to tell me about the different areas of Sydney. I'm not sure why as I haven't asked him for a lowdown of each area. After living in Sydney for a year I like to think I know where most places are.

'So yeah, there's Manly up towards the north and in the south, there is Cronulla…'

After a slight pause, he then completely switches from talking about the suburbs of Sydney to inviting me back to his flat or 'Mansion' as he likes to call it. Still clearly thinks he's a bit of a Hugh Hefner. I feel my heart beat faster, going back to his flat means only one thing and that thing doesn't mean I am going to view his stamp collection. I feel slightly nervous that we are finally going to get together but also really excited, so I continue with the flirty attitude.

'Does your Mansion have a Red Room?'

The confused look on his face makes me laugh out loud.

'You mean the lothario that is Ryan Turner has never read Fifty Shades?'

'Haha surprisingly not, I like to live a life of romance rather than read about it, besides I am no longer a lothario, a certain young lady has changed my view on things…'

'Anyone I know' I ask seductively.

'Maybe'… he replies with a wink… 'I can't give you a red room but I can give you a white room and a rather tasty dinner cooked by yours truly.'

'The dinner sounds perfect although the white room sounds a bit ominous…please explain'. I ask.

'Well you will just have to wait and see won't you'.

He grabs my hand to assist me back up, and after packing our stuff back in our bags we head towards Ryan's flat. I am desperately trying to keep calm but my heart is going at such a speed I'm wondering whether I am going to end up having a cardiac arrest, meaning that again I will miss my chance with Ryan. As you can see I am quite the optimist as to how things pan out in my life.

As we reach Bondi Junction and Ryan's flat, I notice that Ryan's pace has slowed a little and he seems to be taking forever to open the door to his flat.

CHAPTER 28

For the first time as I enter the key in the lock of my flat, I am self-conscious as to what a girl will think of my place. Before it was always a quick in and out and if they didn't like the pile of dirty clothes at the end of the bed or the fact I hadn't cleaned as regularly as I should have it didn't matter as the girl wouldn't be making a return visit. I had no intention for her to stick around and organise me a cleaning rota.

This time it's different. I want this girl to stay. As I let us in, I begin surreptitiously picking up bits and pieces of paper and the random thongs and shoes that are strewn across the floor. I stand cringing at lasts night's dinner plates still left unwashed sitting in the sink and I am really hoping that this doesn't turn Ruby off and she doesn't walk out the door.

'I guess the pixies and fairies didn't get a chance to clean up for you this week Ryan?' she says sarcastically.

'Ah yeah sorry... I should have cleaned up a bit more than I have. I've just been heaps busy with work and stuff and making sure my favourite girl is okay.'

I sweep her perfectly formed body up in my arms and hope my feeble excuse and attempt at a compliment makes up for the tsunami of untidiness that consumes us in the living room.

'Anyways Ruby before I cook dinner would you like to have a look at my white room?'

'Ooh Ryan you are a tease…let me guess it's called the white room because the walls are white like the rest of the flat?'

Dammit she's sussed it out already. Time to win back the situation by plying on the Turner charm a little.

"You are correct Miss Samuels and for that you get a little reward?'

'Excellent…and this reward is?'

'A night in the white room with a personal masseuse, kisser and snuggle buddy by the name of Ryan…'

I smile coyly and kiss her gently on the lips and neck and hear a slight groan part from her lips as I do so. A fire of excitement ignites in her eyes and I think I am starting to get the same feeling in my trousers. It's time to get into this room and devour the beautiful woman in front of me.

As I gently open the door, I stand in shock as to what I see before me.

'Hi Ryan, pleased to see me?

There in front of me is Tanya in a mint green baby doll sprawled all over my bed with her kohl rimmed eyes trying to do their best to get my attention.

I just stand there completely in shock as to what is going on, finally I regain my senses;

'What the fuck are you doing here Tanya? ... How the hell did you get in?'

'Well I hadn't heard from you in a while and I thought I would give you a surprise...aren't you pleased to see me?'

'No I am not, I don't want anything to do with you Tanya now get out and leave before I call the police for breaking and entering.'

My mind is overloaded and confused from all the emotions and questions that are running through my head. And then I realise that Ruby has witnessed the same thing I have. I look for her hand so I know she is there and that I can explain everything to her and how this woman means nothing to me.

Each time I try to grab her hand I get a fistful of air. I take my gaze of anger away from Tanya as she begins to gather her things and I then turn to Ruby with a look of tenderness and desperation. As I turn to face her I see that her beautiful blue eyes are full of tears and anger. In a croaked voice she says;

'Clearly I was mistaken as to who I thought you were....' She turns away and wipes her face with her hands and turns back one last time; 'Goodbye Ryan' and with that parting farewell she heads out of the door and begins to run.

CHAPTER 29

I run as fast as my legs can take me down the apartment block stairs and push my full weight against the fire exit door. The door eventually opens to let me free and as it begins to close again I hear Ryan's voice and it sounds like he said, 'I love you'. I must've misheard. He couldn't have really said that…or did he? I decide there is no point in turning back and I continue to pound down the pavement as the hot Australian sun scorches my back and my face.

'It's time to leave…its time to leave' I begin to mutter to myself, trying to convince my heart that my head is right.

I flag down a cab near Bondi Junction station and try to explain in my best sign language to the taxi driver whose English clearly does not go any further than 'yes' 'no' and 'thank you' that I need to get back to my flat. After several attempts of wild hand gestures and breaking down the words for the driver to understand I feel we are finally getting somewhere and that I might get out of this area.

'Daaahlingggg Harrrrbourrrr'

'Yes you know the one with the water and the boats. It gets very busy, there is a big cinema there too.'

'One with no bridge'

'Yes that's the one, do you know it?'

'I can take you there, no problem'.

Instead of taking a breather in the taxi, I am still on edge as I am left wondering as to whether he does actually understand and know where he is going or whether instead he will end up dropping me in the middle of Darlinghurst instead. So much for making a quick exit.

After what seems like a lifetime, he does finally drop me off at Darling Harbour. I stuff a few notes in his hand and hope its covers the fare and then decide to offer him a small bow as a small mark of respect for getting me to the right destination in one piece.

He shakes his head and mutters to himself 'You English are all the same.' He then puts the taxi back into gear and speeds down the road. I begin to wonder whether I have just been rather insulting to his culture with the mini bow I gave and feel bad for the way I handled the situation. It's not easy to come to another country and start again, I should know… well at least a little bit anyway.

However, more pressing matters await as its time for me to return back home to the wild yet familiar wilderness of the Essex countryside. They do say the only way is Essex and right now it seems like the only and best way to escape all the craziness that has happened in my life over the past few weeks.

I walk towards the apartment which is two blocks from the Harbour and think of what I am going to say to my sister. I know she is going to go bat shit crazy when I tell her that I am leaving and I know she will do her best older twin sister act of convincing me to stay.

As I buzz myself in to the apartment block and head up in the lift, a retching stink fills my nostrils and I see that in the corner of the lift there is a pile of animal faeces…. great just what I wanted to smell and see on my last day in Sydney. I bet you it was that fucking Chihuahua Fifi who decided to use this lift as a toilet. Her owner always seems to be going back and forwards to her accountant to sort out her 'pet grooming' business.

As I turn the key in the apartment door and push it open I see Martha and Chloe curled up on the sofa and I can hear the landlord and his girlfriend playing loud electronic music in their bedroom. Martha jumps up immediately as her twin intuition kicks in as she knows something is not right with me.

I stand in the middle of the living room and announce my declaration to her;

'I am leaving Martha…please don't stop me. I will be packing my clothes and I will be telling that creep of a landlord to go do one and then I will be getting a taxi to the airport to leave this city.'

For a split second we both give each other a stony stare, knowing that a battle will commence of which no one will come out unscathed. However, Martha drops her eyes and then looks back at me like a sad puppy.

'Go Ruby…I will not stop you, we are both adults now and I know you've had a tough time but just tell me one thing, what made you decide to leave now and so abruptly?'

My act of steely composure comes to an end and I can no longer hold back the tears. My body begins to shake as everything erupts from me like a volcano. I tell Martha everything. The good and the bad, it's weird that despite being twins our lives took such different directions whilst in Sydney.

Martha gives me a tight hug which is warm and comforting. I then feel her body become tense and I know that this is a sign that she wants to release some rage...

'That fucking bastard' she spits in my ear... 'If I ever see the guy I will personally kick him in the bollocks for you. I don't want you to leave. I'm also disappointed that you are leaving because of a guy... I thought you would be stronger than this Ruby.'

She releases me from her embrace but holds on tightly to my lower arms so she can look me in the eye and let her disappointment and sadness be fully known to me.

I feel absolutely awful. I do not want to disappoint anybody but I need to stand my ground and prove to her that Ryan is not the maker of my destiny.

'Martha, my decision is not wholly based on a boy, the past few weeks have left me exhausted and being attacked has really shaken me. It is time for me to go home and take stock and get back to being the strong and independent woman I used to be.'

Martha lets out a deep sigh and releases my arms in defeat.

'Okay Ruby, fair enough... it is clear your mind is made up. Let me deal with the landlord as both me and Chloe fancy giving him a good dressing down and we have an eye on an apartment down the road we want to rent anyway. Do you want help in packing your stuff?'

Martha ended up saying the last sentence to the kitchen wall as I had already walked in to our shared bedroom and began stuffing all my clothes into my tatty rucksack. It's amazing that even after a year in Australia I have very little to show for my time except for clothes and a few photos and shells from the various beaches I've visited around the city. I take in all the pictures sitting on my bed side table...Andre and I at Luna Park grinning like loons, a picture of Martha, Chloe and I sitting on Palm Beach licking big ice creams our hair slightly ruffled from the sea breeze and all pretending to look like cool cats with our big sunglasses on. Tess and I pretending we were flower angels wearing big floral headdresses at work. Behind the photo of Tess, I find one of Ryan and me smiling at each other from when we ended up hiding in the Photo Booth to avoid our disastrous dates. I want to throw it away and forget everything with Ryan but for some reason I hide it between the other photos.

After placing the photos on top of the scrumpled clothes in my rucksack with a mixed feeling of warmth and sadness in my stomach, I look out towards the doorway ready to make my exit and I see Martha looking at me with a softness in her face as the sides of her mouth gently lift upwards.

'Oh sis...for just a moment I saw a brief look of happiness on your face when looking at those photos there...it's just a shame you have to go and lose the chance of making some more precious memories here.'

 I try to avoid the subject and keep on track with getting out of this country.

'Okay Martha this is it, I'll get a taxi to the airport and will see if I can get a flight to London today. If not I will try some other Aussie city like Melbourne or something and stay there for a few days until I can get a flight back home.'

Martha comes closer to where I am standing and takes on the role of Mother;

'Now are you sure you have got everything? You do know if you can't get a flight anywhere you can just come back here until things are sorted? Please do be careful Ruby, you've already had one bad experience here, I don't want you to have two. Make sure you text me the details of flights and things once you know…'

'Woah Martha enough with the questions already, your even worse than Mum with all this fussing.'

The soft smile has turned into a smirk and a look of 'don't push your luck.'

'Well you are my little sis even if it is only by three minutes, I have to make sure you are okay…besides Mum would kill me if I hadn't done the mandatory checks on her behalf.' She then winked at me and then gave me another strong hug before helping me lift my fully loaded rucksack on to my slightly pinkish red skin, I knew I should have stuck with the factor 50 rather than the 30.

Whilst I do my best not to moan and groan as the rucksack straps dig into my scorched skin, Martha continues with her instructive tone; 'Right Ruby, me and Chloe will walk you out of the flat and wait with you until you get a taxi and we will do our best to make some fabulous gurning faces to make sure you have a send-off to remember.'

'Thanks so much sis, I couldn't think of a more sentimental and loving way to send off a sister than gurning'.

Then just as we are about to get out of the door Mr Chen makes an appearance from the bedroom and stands in front of us. He is wearing an off-white string vest that covers his podgy stomach along with a pair of rather fetching purple y-fronts. I am not sure whether to laugh or scream at the site of this guy. I do know however that I can finally get my own back on this guy for being such a shit to me before leaving this dump which he advertised to us as a 'perfect haven for temporary city workers'. What we failed to realise was that this was code for a badly worn hidey-hole and a bedroom designed for one is to be shared by three people.

'Hey Mr Chen, good to see you still know how to impress the ladies with those sexy pants on....and that vest, wow...who wouldn't want to rip that off!'

Mr Chen seems confused as to whether I am actually coming on to him or whether I am winding him up.

I see Martha and Chloe trying to stifle their laughs as they push me out of the apartment and into the lifts down to the front entrance in order to prevent me saying any more ludicrous comments to Mr Chen.

I give Martha and Chloe one last strong hug each followed by a kiss on their cheek. I am going to miss them so much. I push my rucksack on the far seat of the taxi and shut the car door. I then wave back at their gurns as I begin my journey to the airport.

CHAPTER 30

I desperately chase after her. I can't let it end like this; 'Ruby…Ruby wait…there's been a mistake…' she's already making progress down the stairwell and I am struggling to keep up with her.

I begin to admit defeat as she is much quicker than I am. I decide that there is only one thing left to do. I shout down the stairwell 'Ruby I love you…' I then hear the fire exit door of the building slam, it's too late she's gone. Distraught, I slump down on the steps in front of me and place my head in my hands.

I then hear a voice I didn't ever want to hear again; 'That is the first time I have ever seen you look at a girl with more than lust in your eyes… I had thought you might eventually care for me that way but clearly it wasn't meant to be…'

'Oh fuck off Tanya'.

She takes her gaze away from me, mutters something under her breath and continues clip-clopping down the stairs in her white platform shoes.

She is right though, this is the first time I actually care about someone. I sit in shock for a few hours on the stairwell as to how I have got into this mess. I try to think of any way I can to get hold of Ruby and explain everything to her and how no one matters except her. I take my phone from my shorts and determinedly ring and ring. It goes to voicemail each time. I eventually leave a message;

'Hi Ruby, its Ryan I know you probably don't want to speak to me right now but I do genuinely love you and I want to see you one more time and tell you I'm sorry. Tanya means nothing to me. Please ring me back.'

I sound pathetic and desperate but I don't care I just need to see her beautiful face, one more time at least.

I try to remember where she said she lived…something about being in an apartment block called Sunshine or maybe it was called Sunrise and that if you head to the rooftop you can see the harbour but not the one with the bridge… Suddenly I have a lightbulb moment…It's got to be one of the apartment blocks in Darling Harbour! I scramble up the stairs and go back to my flat, change into a more presentable shirt and trousers, check my appearance one more time and then run out the door and flag a taxi down and begin to pray that I am travelling to the correct place.

*   *   *

After lots of praying to God, Allah, Buddha and any other religious entity I can think of I finally arrive outside the grey and menacing tower block which has the misleading and friendly name of 'Sunshine Apartments'. I give a generous tip to the taxi driver for putting up with my erratic behaviour and for breaking all the speed limits to get me here and hope that one of the Gods

I prayed to has brought me to the right place.

'Good luck in getting the girl' the driver calls out to me and he speeds off as fast as possible making me unable to make a quick getaway if necessary. As I look through the glass doors of the reception at 'Sunshine Apartments' I see the back of a girl with wavy blonde hair wearing a short purple sun dress heading towards the lifts up into the apartment with another girl who has short black hair. I recognise Ruby's wavy hair instantly but she is wearing a different outfit…she must have changed. I begin to pound on the glass 'Ruby…Ruby. It's me Ryan, can we talk.'

As she turns around my heart sinks a little as it isn't Ruby, it's her twin sister. I know it is her twin as Martha doesn't have the scar that poor Ruby has. Although maybe she can help me get to Ruby.

'It's Martha, isn't it?!' I yell at the glass.

She looks at me wide eyed with confusion.

'My names Ryan and I know your sister Ruby. I really need to get hold of her right now…'

Cautiously, she walks towards the glass doors and lets me in to the foyer. Once inside she gives me a well-deserved face full of venom.

'So you are the Ryan that has just broke my sister's heart, I have a right mind to kick you in the bollocks for what you have just done to her.'

I cross my legs instinctively. 'Martha please don't do that, let me explain what has happened…' I go through the whole story of how I first met Ruby and up to the point of her fleeing from my arms just a few hours earlier.

After the explanation of my tragic love life she pauses for a moment and then mutters under her breath;

'And people wonder why I became a lesbian. Men are just too much hard work…'

She then moves closer to my face and I can see the same look of strength and determination in her blue eyes as her sister and as her warm breath beats against my face as she tell me news the I didn't want to hear.

'Ryan despite your previous actions you seem like a good bloke but I am afraid she's gone to the airport. She is going back home. Australia has given her some very high highs but also some very low lows and to be honest she is exhausted from it all. I'm sorry Ryan you're just a little bit too late. She's gone.'

'No, no, no…it can't end like this…' I yell to myself, in the hope that the continued repetition will release me from the nightmare of today.

Martha then interrupts my cries of desperation by pulling out a scrumpled piece of paper from her shoulder bag and begins scrawling on it from a chewed blue biro left at the reception desk. 'Here lover boy…this might help.' She hands me the tattered paper which has an address of a place in Essex.

'What is this for?' I ask perplexed.

'It's our address back home in Epping Forest, it's near London. If you are that madly in love with her send her a letter, she is more likely to read it than a text or online message as she won't know it's from you until she opens it. And knowing Ruby the curiosity will get the better of her and she will want to know how you tracked her down.'

I give Martha a massive hug and hold on tight knowing that

there is still a glimmer of hope. Eventually Martha begins to push me away.

'Jeez Dude if you squeeze me any tighter I am going to burst, and you don't want to piss my sister off any further knowing that you nearly suffocated me!'

She sees that I don't quite know whether she is being serious or not and she bursts out laughing.

'Cheer up Ryan it isn't the end of the world, both you and my sister will see the funny side of this one day...'

I say my goodbyes to Martha and thank her for her help and begin the long walk to Lavender Bay to visit the only person who can help me sort out my life right now.

It's time to visit Mum.

*   *   *

An hour later, I finally arrive outside 14 Northcutt Avenue, Lavender Bay and I am greeted not only by the traditional white picket fence but also by the god forsaken creature that is Larry, sunbathing on the front lawn in just his white y-fronts. He has clearly been there a while as his normally pale white body is starting to turn a rather deep pink. Normally at this point I would shout out some scathing remark but I feel too hot and bothered from the long walk in the blaring sun and too emotionally drained to say anything to him except asking where Mum is.

'She's in her study...currently writing her next book... the doors unlocked so you can walk straight through...mate are you okay? Your eyes look all puffy and bloodshot....'

I completely ignore Larry and head to Mum's study.

'Hello Ryan' she says chirpily. 'I could hear my darling Larry speaking to you outside. Just wait one moment as I am on the last sentence of my book, 'How to Move on From Your Man...'

With a final flourish of her fountain pen, she turns around from her mahogany desk in her green swivel leather chair, places her half-moon rimmed glasses on her head and stands up. She looks at me in shock.

'Oh Ryan, come here, tell me exactly what has happened. You look terrible.' I hold my Mum tight to my chest as if I am a little boy again.

I breathe in her deep damask perfume and begin to sob. In between gulping for air and using my Mum's top as a make do tissue, I tell her why I have become a tearful mess;

'I've fallen in love Mum and now the girl I'm in love with has gone.'

She takes a step back and grabs me by the arms and looks directly into my eyes with a look of fire and protectionism.

'Now now Ryan you are a strong man and I don't like to see you get upset, whatever has happened between you and this girl I am sure can be fixed, and if there is no way this romance can be fixed I highly recommend you read my book and replace every reference of 'Man' with 'Woman'.

I look at her in sheer disbelief that during my time of turmoil she is trying to flog her next book to her son. I need my Mum not Dr. Lara Turner the celebrity psychologist.

After seeing my confused and hurt face, she bursts into a hearty laugh; 'I'm only joking Ryan, let's go into the kitchen and have some tea and cake and you can fill me in on the whole story and we can work out what to do next. And I promise not to refer to my book or any of my other publications during our conversation.'

This is Mum's solution to everything, a good cup of tea and a decent piece of cake. It's a family tradition back from when she was growing up in the UK. Apparently, her Grandmother refused to solve any family problems until everyone had eaten a slice of cake and had a cup of tea. I am surprised our family isn't riddled with diabetes.

Larry suddenly skips in to the kitchen gleaning for attention. I really do not need this guy to sit their grinning whilst I wallow in my own misery and telling Mum how much of a fool I have been. Luckily Mum has her 'Ryan needs some alone time with Mum' radar on full beam and gives him something to do.

'Larry be a doll would you and head to the shops to get me some more cake, I think Ryan and I will probably finish the last of the coconut and cherry I have, and you know how miserable I get if there isn't enough cake in the house...'

Larry does as he is told and heads to the landing where he grabs his shorts and thankfully a t-shirt to cover up the red lobster look he is sporting underneath before making his way to the front door.

If it was me I would have told him to do something too but it ends in off and really isn't a nice thing to say in the company of others.

After devouring the door slab slice of cherry and coconut cake and slurping my Earl Grey, I fill Mum in on the whole situation. After talking it through I feel slightly better and more optimistic that I can win Ruby back knowing that I have her address in England and can write to her and hopefully convince her to come back and start again.

I eagerly look at Mum to see what her response will be and how I can work at winning her back. She takes a sharp intake of breath and I already know she isn't going to give me the answer I want to hear.

'Well Ryan, in my honest opinion I think you should give this girl some space. A lot has happened to both of you over the past few months and I think you both need some time away from each other, and that includes time apart in the virtual and letter writing world too. This is the first time I have seen you this besotted about a girl and I want to make sure that you are doing the right thing Ryan. Focus on you for a bit, besides what's love but a second-hand emotion?'

'Firstly Mum, did you just quote me a Tina Turner song? Secondly, I really don't see the harm in sending her a letter, besides what with it needing to go all the way to England it will be a couple of weeks until she would get it and I really don't want to lose this girl and for her to think that I am douchebag by not getting in contact.'

She sighs heavily, 'Well Ryan all the communication methods you have tried so far haven't grabbed her attention. What makes you think she will respond to your letter after just a couple of weeks back in the UK where she will still be processing her time in Australia and working out what to do next. Give it time Ryan. Time is a good healer. Both you and Ruby need time to become strong loving individuals again. If you both still feel the same in a few months' time you can put your all in the relationship and the bond between you will be tighter and more solid than before as you've spent time reflecting and working out what you want... and by the way I did quote you a bit of 'What's Love Got To Do With It' from the legend that is Tina Turner. If Tina can look at love in a more objective way then I am sure you can too Ryan', she then chuckles to herself and winks in my direction.

Knowing that I am still not quite convinced by her approach, she touches my hand in a comforting way as she continues with her sensible lecture mode as to what to do next in my love life.

'Be strong Ryan, I know you will get through these next few months, besides in three months' time I am actually off to the UK for a three-week book tour. Unfortunately my beautiful snuggle puppy Larry is booked up to perform as a dancer in Madame Butterfly at the Sydney Opera House so he won't be able to join me…soooo…I am going to need a new travel partner…are you up for it? It would mean that if your feelings for this girl are still as strong as they are now you can send her that letter in person which would be much more romantic than sending it through the post. So what do ya say Ryan?'

'I'm in.' I reply assertively.

'Excellent, I'll sort out your flights and stuff and in the meantime spend some quality time reflecting on what you really want from life.'

Sometimes there is an upside to having a Mum who is a psychology professor even if she does have a boyfriend who she refers to as a 'snuggle puppy'.

Three months feels like an eternity right now, as I want to hold Ruby now and tell her how much she means to me but as much as I hate saying it, Mum is right, we both need time to breathe and digest the relationship we have had. I know my feelings won't change for her in the coming months. Besides it will give me time to do something I never thought before, which is to come to terms with the feeling of love instead of the feelings of lust.

CHAPTER 31

Well this isn't quite how I expected my trip to Australia to end. I was hoping for a big group of friends I would've have met on my travels in Australia to see me and my sister off back home with lots of hugs and smiles and promises of visits to see them all. Martha and I would then skip into departures and begin planning our next trip to Australia and how we will one day make Paradise our home.

Instead I am on my own, emotionally exhausted from everything this country has thrown at me. The situation isn't helped by the fact I have just had to do battle with the Barbie doll look alike behind the British Airways desk to get a flight. Thankfully her acrylic nails managed to tap some magic keys and find me a seat on to the next flight to London via Dubai due to a last-minute cancellation.

As I sit by the gate waiting to return to old Blighty, I do my best to avoid the irritating little boy who is going up and down the gangways on his wheely suitcase that's in the shape of a unicorn.

'Go Sparky...Go!' shouts the toddler as he veers very close to my legs. I swear to God if he runs over my foot with that fucking suitcase I will put Sparky the Unicorn so far up that child's backside he will have something to shout about. Knowing my luck, I'll be sitting next to this Terror Toddler for the whole journey home.

Whilst trying to avoid an amputated foot, I think about my time in Australia and also Ryan.

I have learnt a lot during my time here and not just that drop bears don't exist. The first is that there is more to life than sitting at a desk. Having the opportunity to try something different and learn the basic skills of floristry and also being able to publish my illustrations has made me more determined than ever to have a career that is not 9-5. I also met lots of interesting people and will miss not being able to have random catch ups with Andre, making jokes with the customers at 'Fascinating Florals' and sharing my dating disasters with Tess, Martha and Chloe and eating my body weight in Tim Tams.

I will also miss the weather even though it's not always as perfect as the travel brochures told me. Despite the incident on Bondi beach, I still love the beaches of Sydney and being able to hear sound of the waves crashing on the shore and watching all the surfers bob about in the water whilst the runners go past them leaving imprints in the wet sand.

I won't however miss having to share my personal space with everybody and I won't miss Vegemite as Marmite rules no matter what any Aussie tells you and I won't, despite my heart telling me otherwise, miss Ryan.

I begin to wonder whether I really did fall in love with Ryan or just had a bad case of lust. After seeing Tanya writhing on his bed I am just totally confused as to whether he felt any love towards me at all or whether it was just a game to him as to see how far he could go with a loved up Pommie.

Looking back its been an adventure full of highs and lows, although I doubt Disney will be making a film about my life anytime soon.

When I get back home I intend to make a promise to myself not to take life too seriously and to stop looking for love as it is causing me more pain than joy. Now it is time to not give a care in the world about feelings and just lust rather than love...Ryan seems to have coped perfectly well with lusting rather than loving...

And as I let out an audible sigh, I hear the tannoy announcement tell me it's time to board my flight.

I jump to my feet and join the boarding pass queue, my heart beating unexpectedly fast in my chest. This is it. My time in Australia is up. I look at the scar on my arm and shudder knowing that the attack could have been a lot worse if it wasn't for Ryan. The scar is also a reminder of how precious life is and that I need to grab and go for any opportunity I can.

Once boarded I walk quickly to the plane to prevent me having second thoughts and returning back to a land that was filled with so much promise. I do my best not to make eye contact with the perfectly dressed air hostess at the plane door so she cannot see my feeble attempts to screw up my face to stop the big fat tears rolling down my slightly sunburnt cheeks.

The feeling of sadness does not last long as I notice that a unicorn case is being placed into the luggage compartment above where I am about to be seated. It looks like I will be spending the next twenty-four hours thinking of different ways to kill the Terror Toddler and make it look like an accident. I let out another deep sigh, place my bag in the compartment also and pull my phone from the back pocket of my jeans in order to switch it to flight mode before we take off.

On the screen I notice that amongst the several voice mails and texts from Ryan several hours ago, I have a message from Laurence. I'd almost forgotten about Laurence during my time with Ryan. Although we did keep in touch throughout my time in Oz, even after he went back to the UK after doing his farm work several months ago.

I open the message to read it fully and feel my heart beginning to pound again. I excitedly turn my phone off and put it back in my rucksack and sit down in my seat knowing that even the Terror Toddler next to me won't be able to dampen my mood now. There is a new adventure that awaits in the UK and I cannot wait for it to begin.

STEPHANIE CROSS

ACKNOWLEDGEMENTS

A big thank you to my parents Denise and Andrew who have encouraged and believed in my writing even when I doubted myself. And Dad, "You can, you can, you can my son!!" Also to my brother Rob; don't forget your sister when you are earning lots of P!

A super massive thank you to the handsome and mysterious Duke, who has had to listen to me continuously talk about my hopes and fears in writing this book. Throughout you have remained, patient, calm and just truly amazing. I look forward to our future adventures together.

Ashleigh and Steph, thank you for ensuring my time in Australia was an adventure I will never forget.

Also a thanks to Susan Harrison who helped edit this book and to Jessica Bell, for creating such an awesome cover.

ABOUT THE AUTHOR

Ever since she learned how to read, Stephanie has loved books, so much so that she decided to begin writing her own books full of fun, love and adventure.

Stephanie has written for a variety or publications in a non-fiction capacity, both in the UK and Australia and is keen to venture further into the world of fiction.

When not putting pen to paper you can find her trying to grapple with the law or stuffing her face with chocolate buttons.

To keep up to date with the latest news and publications from Stephanie Cross, connect via the following channels:

Twitter: @stephiecross1

Web: www.itsdefinitelystephanie.com

Lightning Source UK Ltd.
Milton Keynes UK
UKHW011813060619
343981UK00001B/60/P